A Mantra for Miss Perfect

A Mantra for Miss Perfect

A Sood Family Romance

Sapna Srinivasan

A Mantra for Miss Perfect
Copyright© 2023 Sapna Srinivasan
Tule Publishing First Printing, January 2023

The Tule Publishing, Inc.

ALL RIGHTS RESERVED

First Publication by Tule Publishing 2023

Cover design by Lee Hyat Designs

No part of this book may be used or reproduced in any manner whatsoever without written permission except in the case of brief quotations embodied in critical articles and reviews.

This is a work of fiction. Names, characters, places, and incidents are products of the author's imagination or are used fictitiously. Any resemblance to actual events, locales, organizations, or persons, living or dead, is entirely coincidental.

ISBN: 978-1-958686-71-3

Dedication

For Shyam and Noyonika Srinivasan.

Chapter One

IT WAS SAHANA Sood's favorite mistake—weekend yoga with her mom, Sharmila Sood. And like all mistakes, this too began with a good intention—a gift card for a month of lessons at The Lumi Yoga Studio. Her mother had insisted the gift would remain incomplete unless Sahana came along. "Like chai without samosa," she had added for effect. At the time, the request had appeared harmless. *Harmless.*

"Stupid, stupid, stupid," Sahana muttered under her breath, plodding onto her yoga mat while her mom set up next to her.

"You still haven't told me why you went to see your OB-GYN last week," her mom said, as she centered herself on her mat. "It wasn't your annual check, because that happened a few months ago."

"Take a deep breath in, as we begin our full body flow," came Penny Dalla's swami voice. She was a gorgeous blonde with a perfect yoga body—tight abs, tight butt, tight everything. "Get your energy flowing, actively channeling it into Tadasana or Mountain Pose, starting with your feet, to your calves, to your thighs, to your hips, your waist, breathe out and in again, as your pull your stomach muscles into your spine, remembering to breathe in deep—"

"Sahana?" her mom whispered, leaning closer to her. "Why won't you tell me?"

"It was just a regular visit," Sahana whispered back as Penny's calming voice continued to flow through the room.

"Close your eyes if you want to or leave them open. Derive your intentionality as you fold your hands to your heart in Anjuli Mudra…"

"But there's something you're not telling me," her mother insisted.

Sahana closed her eyes and breathed in deep. "I wanted to talk to her—my OB-GYN—about my options."

"Inhale, yogis, let your breath comb through your body from head to toe."

"Options for what?" her mother asked.

"Stand by yourself, through the practice as we move our arms down, touch the flat of both palms to the ground, with them resting side by side next to your feet, bend your knees, ground your palms, and one leg at a time, stretch out to Plank Pose, like so."

Sahana followed Penny's instructions to a tee, with her mother reluctantly following suit. "For freezing my eggs," she replied in a flat voice.

The words instantly caused her mother to surrender her Whatever Pose. She sat up on her haunches. "What? What did you say? Freezing your—"

"Mom, really, it's no big deal," Sahana said, as she continued to hold her plank before transitioning into Cow Pose, led by Penny's voice.

Her mother frowned hard. "Not a big deal? It is the most bullshit idea I have ever heard."

There appeared to be a pause in the room. Sahana, who was by now immersed in Downward Dog, lifted her head up briefly to eye her mother as a few heads turned around to look at them before turning away. To the outside world, her mother was the quintessential Indian auntie, the matriarch of the Sood family, following the death of Sahana's paternal grandmother. In the family's eyes, Sharmila Sood was poised and traditional. But behind the curtains, where there remained no witnesses, her mother tended to curse like a bridezilla. Sahana let out a sigh. Capitulating her pose, she sank into crossed legs on her yoga mat. "It's not bullshit," she said, locking eyes with the older woman. "I'm thirty-two, single, without the slightest *hint* of the whereabouts of my Mr. Right. I need to be realistic with myself."

Her mother shook her head as her eyes softened. "Sahana, God has given you everything. You're beautiful, you're smart, you're a great cook, you love kids, you're respectful of our traditions—"

"And yet, somehow, I can't find a husband," Sahana stated plainly. This was, after all, the bottom line. It wasn't as if she hadn't tried. It wasn't as if she didn't *want* to get married. She loved the idea of starting a family of her own—a husband, kids, mommy groups, and visits to the Hindu temple down the block. She'd been brought up to believe that was where the river ended. Without that piece in place, her life felt unfinished. And she was supposed to be the overachieving cousin. The Sood who'd nailed success in all the relevant aspects of Indian-American life—career, money, upholding traditional values. That was the image she'd lived up to all these years, and yet, every single underachieving cousin of hers had managed to race past her in the love department. They were all married, either happily or unhappily, with babies and baby bumps, hither and thither.

"So, if you can't find a husband, you're going to put your eggs in a cold freezer? Is that your solution?" her mother asked.

"No, it's not a solution. It's a plan. A backup in case things...I don't know, if I don't find a man, I can at least have a child. I've had this on my mind for a while, and I wanted to put it into motion. I'm tired of waiting," Sahana said, turning to watch the others enter Savasana. "I think we should continue." She gestured to Penny who was giving them both the stink eye.

Turning around, Sahana lay flat on her back on her mat and closed her eyes. She did what Savasana entailed—entered a Corpse Pose. Her mother gingerly followed, but she was clearly in no mood to play the game.

"You may be tired of waiting, but I am not tired of trying, Sahana. I don't want microwave-grandbabies," she snapped, resting her head on her mat, and closing her eyes while retaining a deep-set frown.

But this caused her daughter to sit back up. "Please don't tell me you've got more boys for me to meet?" she asked, pleadingly. This had gone on for almost five years. Five years of meeting eligible Indian bachelors at varying locations, only to discover they were eligible morons. When they weren't morons, the few that she'd liked, had been uninterested in her. One of them, Hari Singh, a handsome doctor from a wealthy Seattle family had ended up falling for one of her cousins, Laila Sood.

That one really took the cake.

"I have four lined up and I will send you a text with their pictures," her mother replied. "And Sahana, I'm telling you I have a feeling about one of them. I have a feeling he's the one."

"Uh-huh," Sahana nodded. "So, do I still need to meet the other three, then?"

Her mother shot her a frown. "Mohanji has said they are all good matches for you."

"*All* good, huh? Mohanji said?" Sahana frowned. Mohanji was their trusted family astrologer—trusted to consistently deliver bullshit predictions. And yet, not a single marriage, or a single match ever occurred in the Sood family without his approval. He was like the side salad one ordered with a burger—customary, but wholly useless.

WHEN YOGA ENDED, Sahana and her mom rolled up their mats and walked out of the studio together. She was always left feeling the same way, after each weekend session—like she'd endured a slow, painful death.

"Let's at least get lunch together?" her mom said, as they neared the parking lot.

Sahana shook her head. "I can't. I've got to prepare for a meeting I have tomorrow with George Yoland, one of the managing partners at the firm." While finding a husband was well outside of her control, Sahana had always held the reins on her career nice and tight. It was what gave her comfort on those cold, dark nights. While the rest of the world celebrated Valentine's Day and wedding anniversaries, she spooned her legal files and client decks. Plus, it provided her the perfect alibi at family gatherings overflowing with curious relatives asking why she wasn't married yet. "Oh, I'm too busy with my career to find a husband. I'm a lawyer." Mic drop.

At present, her sights were set on a promotion to junior partner at her firm, Yoland and Wiseman—a goal she felt was within reach, considering she'd managed to close multiple acquisition deals that quarter for their largest client—well, except that one deal that had evaded her and which was likely to come up in her meeting the next day.

"Okay, but remember, next weekend is our Rakhi celebration."

"Oh, right," Sahana said. She'd forgotten it was. Raksha Bandhan, also called Rakhi, was an Indian festival that celebrated a sister's relationship with a brother, or any brotherly figure. Sisters generally tied a sacred thread around the wrist of anyone they regarded as a brother or who they believed offered them protection and love. Rakhi was hugely celebrated in the Sood household, regardless of whether or not there was any brotherly or sisterly love lost.

"You know everyone will be there, including Laila, Hari, Mira, and Andy," her mom continued to say. "Have you spoken to Shaan?" she added.

Sahana shook her head. Shaan Sood was her first cousin, once removed. He was tall, handsome, thirty-three years old, married with a six-year-old daughter, Misha. Sahana and he were close. She was closer to him than the other cousins because Shaan and she had grown up together. They'd lived in the same neighborhood, gone to the same school and even shared a few teachers along the way. But Shaan had been living in India the past few years, moving there after his marriage to his painter wife, Anita. But about a month ago, he'd returned to Seattle with only his daughter, and no one knew why. Not even his parents.

"I was going to go see him after work tomorrow," Sahana said, pulling her clicker out to unlock her blue E-Class Benz.

"Tell him about Rakhi," her mom said. "He has to be there, and so do you."

Sahana reached forward and hugged her mother. "I will," she replied.

SAHANA LIVED IN Downtown Kirkland near Marina Park, in a swanky community that overlooked the gorgeous Juanita Beach. It was a checkbox and she had checked it. Social status meant everything in the Sood family. What one made and how they made it, determined their pecking order in the community and by extension, the power of influence they held within it. Successfully placed children meant their parents received not only respect but the right to give others advice without notice or solicitation, a.k.a. her mother's dream job in life.

Placing her Lululemon yoga bag on a side table, Sahana walked over to her refrigerator and grabbed herself some sparkling water. She slipped out to her balcony and sat down in one of the two chairs. Her eyes slowly grazed over to the empty seat next to her as she sipped the fizzy drink. The seat felt emptier to her than it looked. It was ironic, really. To the rest of the world, she was Miss Perfect. She had it all. What she wasn't born with, she had achieved through hard work. She'd ruthlessly chased her goals in life and overcome obstacles big and small along the way. Sure, to some she came across as nothing short of a badass bitch. And maybe she was, in some ways, in some instances, where a badass bitch was required to be present. But no one, not even her mother knew what it was like to be Sahana Sood—to walk a tightrope all your life without ever breathing oxygen, and without a partner to lean on for balance, or comfort.

Sahana pulled her knees to her chest and closed her eyes to the gentle wind that blew her hair away from her face. Her thoughts drifted to her meeting the next day. If she could get that promotion, she promised herself she'd take a vacation, maybe even a sabbatical. Husband or no husband, the promotion would be her consolation prize.

Standing up from her seat, Sahana headed back indoors to retrieve her laptop so she could work on her reports. Ten minutes of wallowing in self-pity was all she could afford at the moment. She needed the meeting with her boss to go well the next day.

Chapter Two

HER ALARM WOKE her up at five A.M. It had since she was twenty-one. And her morning routine hadn't changed one bit since then. She woke up, brushed her teeth, showered, blow-dried her hair, put her makeup on, got dressed in the clothes she'd laid out the night before. This time, it was a navy tweed skirt, satin gray top, and a matching jacket. She grabbed her coffee, ate some cereal for breakfast, brushed again, flossing this time, headed out the door.

She'd moved out of her parents' waterfront home on Lake Sammamish when she turned eighteen and headed off to the University of Washington. She'd gotten into UCLA, too, but her mother insisted she stay close to home. The program at UCLA had been better, more to her liking. But nothing, absolutely nothing, could win against her mother's wishes. Not in Sahana's world. So, she'd ended up choosing Washington. She stayed on campus, however. She was mama's girl, sure. But not self-destructive.

College had been liberating—*educational* as far as men were concerned. She'd dated around, mostly men from her Indian-American community, so as not to offend her mother. She'd also worked her butt off on her law degree, which was really a no-choice choice in her world. It was either law or medicine, so she'd chosen courtroom drama over blood drama.

PULLING INTO THE underground gated parking lot in downtown Seattle, Sahana rode the elevator to the twenty-first floor and her office at Yoland and Wiseman. She heard her stilettos *clickety-clacking* against the polished floors as she walked through the open glass doors. It led straight to the reception desk, where Marissa Van Carlson, the receptionist, offered her a welcoming smile followed by, "Good morning."

Sahana smiled back. Her eyes glanced upward to the large chrome lettering on the wall behind Marissa that read: LAW OFFICES OF YOLAND AND WISEMAN.

Sublime. The experience of walking into a swanky office in the heart of Seattle, knowing she'd earned her place in it fair and square almost made up for the things Sahana lacked in her personal life—a husband, a family, and all the bragging rights that tradition afforded with it. She felt it every morning as she walked through those doors, past the clear glass cubicles, the polished maple floors, the dark built-in bookshelves, and those sexy corner offices that offered the best views of the city, making one feel on top of the world even if they weren't in reality. Or maybe it was that she'd made it a point to remind herself of it. Of what she had versus what she didn't. *Who needs a husband, dummy? Look at this, shit.*

Making her way down the hallway, Sahana walked past some conference rooms to her south-facing cubicle that derived the best of the morning light without any of the greenhouse effects. Offloading her laptop bag onto the floor and her travel coffee mug onto her desk, she unpacked her laptop, plugging it into her large double-monitors.

"You really are dressed for success, today," came a familiar voice, causing Sahana to look up. Her eyes fell upon her legal assistant, James Ware.

"Says the man in the bow tie and vest." She smiled back.

James was one of her closest friends and confidants in the office. He was a man of medium stature, with soft blue eyes, and peachy-white skin. They'd known each other over six years and she'd even been a bridesmaid at his wedding to his then-partner-now-husband, Ethan Fray.

"What, *this*?" James asked, with an effective twirl. "This is a celebration outfit."

Sahana frowned. "Celebration of what?"

"Of the moment I bought the bow tie and vest at Nordstrom yesterday."

Sahana laughed, shaking her head. "Ethan's going to shred that credit card if you're not careful."

"Who's shredding what?" came the voice of Candace Hope, the firm's senior marketing manager, as she popped her head in the door, behind James.

"Sahana thinks I'm a shopaholic and I'm trying to convince her it's gay pride," James said, plainly.

Candace nodded. "Got it." She was a tall woman with platinum-blonde hair that perfectly complemented her white skin, gray eyes, and plumped-pink lips. Candace and Sahana had met back in college when she was a marketing major and Sahana was studying to be a lawyer. They'd stayed in touch and eventually found their way into the same law firm when she'd referred Candace to the firm's recruiting team.

James walked over to sit down in one of the two chairs across the desk from Sahana while Candace settled into a couch a few feet away.

"I take it you're prepared for your meeting with George, today?" Candace asked, as she watched Sahana typing away on her computer.

She nodded. "Prepared as ever. I've been working my butt off on these deals for Doubledown Resorts."

"The resort chain that likes to acquire small inns and turn them into money-making things?" Candace asked, to which Sahana nodded.

"And they're our firm's largest client," James added, crossing his legs. "Sahana's managed to close five out of six acquisitions deals for them."

"Geez. What happened to the sixth one?" Candace asked, with mock concern.

"The Wildling Inn," Sahana said, keeping her eyes on her monitor while her fingers worked independently on the keyboard. *The one that got away.* It was a beautiful Gig Harbor property on which Doubledown had its heart set. "It's run by an older couple, Clive and Sigi Harring. Their nephew, Ryan Mehra owns the inn, however. He inherited the place when his parents died six years ago. We spoke a few times on the phone, and he showed great interest at first...everything seemed so perfectly aligned, given he lives and works in New York, and his aunt and uncle who've been running the business are nearing retirement. But he pulled out all of a sudden," Sahana said.

"Ryan Mehra, huh?" Candace frowned. "He sounds Indian. And *young*."

Sahana shrugged. "He's thirty-three. His father was Indian, his mother's white. He's an only child, but he has numerous cousins. His parents met in college, dated a year before getting married. Following that, his parents bought ten acres in Gig Harbor back in the eighties along with the dilapidated nineteenth-century house that stood on it, which they restored and called The Wildling Inn. Ryan himself isn't active on social media, hasn't updated his timelines anywhere, except on LinkedIn. And he's got no pictures of himself anywhere, either, except for one we found of him, in a high school yearbook. He went to the University of Washington, and moved to New York right after his parents passed away and is a senior product manager at a tech company…Blue Tech. He's into bike racing and had his last one at the Mac Quint Velodrome in Redmond, when he visited the inn three months ago, and er, he's allergic to pistachios."

Candace's eyes widened. "Wow. You know more about him than I do about my boyfriend."

James frowned. "Hey, don't give Sahana all the credit. I uncovered the part about the pistachios."

Sahana smiled. "You know what they say about acquisition deals…due diligence, due diligence—"

"Due diligence," Candace and James joined in together for the third chorus.

"How do you think old George will react to your saga

about The Wildling Inn slipping your net?" Candace asked.

"Not as well as you did." Sahana sighed. "I'm not thrilled about it. It's not *perfect*. But it's not the end of the world that Ryan changed his mind. It happens."

Candace appeared thoughtful. "Will this impact your promotion, do you think?"

Sahana felt her heart skip a beat at the question, but she maintained a perfectly placid exterior. "Of course not. George knows how hard I work for the firm. He knows the millions I've pulled in, not just for Doubledown, but over the years. He knows. And I'll be sure to highlight the fact at our meeting today."

"Sahana's got her ducks in a row," James confirmed with a nod. "She always does."

Sahana smiled back. "Only because I like them in a row."

GEORGE YOLAND, CO-FOUNDER, and managing partner at Yoland and Wiseman was a man of few words. He'd practiced law for two thirds of his life and was on the road to retirement. All the more reason Sahana needed to get that promotion. If George were to leave, she had no idea who'd take his place. Whoever it was, she'd have to start from scratch with them to prove her worth before even the mention of a promotion.

Standing outside his glass cubicle, she administered a gentle knock on the door. Inside, she could see George on the phone as he gestured for her to come in. Entering the room, she walked over to sit down in the chair across the large desk from him. A moment later, he signed off from his call. "My apologies, that was my dentist's office. Apparently I need my wisdom teeth removed."

Sahana rolled her eyes. "That's how they do it. They first extract our wisdom, then they take our money."

George coughed up a laugh. "Right, Miss Sood. Let's talk about you and all the great work you've been doing these past months."

A fair start. Sahana smiled. "I gather you looked over the report I sent you?"

George laughed and casually flipped through some printed pages before him. "I did. And I'm impressed at the finesse you've shown in closing these deals for Doubledown."

"Thank you, George…"

"But this one, here, The Wildling Inn. What happened with that one?"

Sahana's confidence quivered but she regained herself. "Right, I know Doubledown was highly inclined toward acquiring that property, but the owner appears to have changed his mind. He went dark a few weeks ago and hasn't been returning any of my calls or emails."

George nodded. "Do we know why?"

Sahana shook her head. "It wasn't for lack of effort on our part. We worked hard on it…James, especially. He helped uncover some key elements relating to er, pista—well, the owner's, er, internal algorithm."

George massaged his chin, tentatively. "You know, my wife and I've been married, forty-three years. And just yesterday, I discovered she drinks an extra cup of coffee on Wednesdays. *Just* Wednesdays. Because that's the day she has her rotating book club meetings."

"Right." Sahana grappled with this information, wondering about George's point.

"You see, there's never a limit to how much you can discover about a person, or a situation."

Ah. Sahana smiled. "I totally agree, George. And I'll continue to passively follow up with Ryan. He may not be interested in selling, but that doesn't mean he won't ever sell."

George nodded. "Pity it fell through. It would've made a better case with the board for your promotion if we'd had this one in the bag along with the others."

Sahana felt herself stiffen. She said nothing as George continued.

"Of course, the board knows you're a strong contender for the position. But so is Walter Cruz, who, as you know, has had his fair share of successes in the short time he's been with us."

Sahana swallowed hard. "Yes, I'm aware." Walter Cruz was the lawyer version of a great white shark. A younger, feistier, golf-playing, partner-schmoozing shark. He'd been with the firm just a few years—not nearly as long as she had, but already, he was vying for the same promotion as she was. It was moments like these that reminded her she was a woman, living in a man's world. "I'm very much aware," she said again, as if to herself this time.

"Still," George said, flipping through the pages of the report. "I think you've done well, and I'm sure the board will be pleased with the result."

Sahana nodded absently. "Great, thank you, I'm glad."

She wasn't listening anymore. She was thinking—about Ryan Mehra, The Wilding Inn, and about Walter Cruz spinning in a large swivel chair in the junior partner's office.

Chapter Three

WHEN HER MEETING with George wrapped up, Sahana marched past her cubicle down to James's desk in the open bullpen. "What does the rest of my day look like today?" she asked him, when she was close enough to accommodate a whisper.

James turned to his monitor. "You have some internal one-on-one meetings and some follow-up client calls you need to make."

"Reschedule the meetings, but not the calls. I can take those from the car," she said with urgency.

James looked up at her. "Wait, are you leaving for somewhere?"

"*We* are, yes. We're driving to The Wilding Inn," Sahana said.

"The Wilding Inn?" James frowned. "But I thought the team wasn't actively pursuing it anymore? Weren't we going to wait for Ryan to get back to us to see if he wants to reengage?"

"I know, I know, I just…I need to understand what happened, James. I want to give it one last try. If I can't get to Ryan, then I want to try my luck with his aunt and uncle—get a foot in the door. It's not a clear shot, but it's a chance, and"—Sahana lowered her voice—"it's a tipping point that could affect my promotion."

James's eyes widened. "Did George say that?"

"He implied it," Sahana said.

James sighed. "How about I meet you in the lobby in ten minutes?"

Sahana nodded. Turning, she began walking away. "Eight. Meet me in eight minutes," she amended, tossing the words over her shoulder.

Back in her office, she sent out a couple of last-minute emails, before gathering her laptop bag. Her cell phone rang just as she exited her office. It was her mom. "Hey, Mom. Look, I can't talk right now…"

"Can't talk? What do you mean? I'm not one of your clients, I'm your mother who gave you the gift of life."

Sahana sighed. "Okay, could you at least make it quick?"

"I'm calling to remind you to stop by your cousin Shaan's house this evening. Don't forget, no matter how busy you are, okay?"

"Yeah, I'll remember," Sahana said quickly.

"He is your cousin and we haven't heard a word from him since he moved back from India. His mother has barely spoken to him or her grandchild since they returned," her mother continued. "You know she came by for lunch today? She was weeping. She was so sad she didn't even compliment my cooking like she always does."

Sahana arrived at the lobby and caught James approaching in the distance.

"Are you even listening?" her mother asked, fervently.

"Yeah, yup. I er—I caught every word, and I will strive

to be the best daughter in the world, but right now I've got to go, Mom. I'll check in on Shaan after work today, okay? Promise."

Her mother let out a second sigh. "Fine, okay. Bye."

James arrived with a smile. "I take it that was your ever-loving mother?"

"Ever-fretting, you mean?" she said, turning to face the reception desk. "Marissa, could you send these out by express mail today, please? I've got sticky notes on them with the addresses for each one."

"Sure, I'll take care of it," Marissa said with a smile, accepting the documents.

"Can I ask you a question, boss?" James asked, as they began walking down the hallway toward the elevator.

Sahana punched the elevator button. "Sure. But make it a good one."

"What happens if you can't get your foot in the door with Ryan's aunt and uncle? What then?"

Sahana breathed in, as the elevator door opened for them. "I'll cross that bridge when I get to it."

THE WILDLING INN stood at the very end of a long, tree-lined driveway. The property sat on ten acres of land along the harbor waterfront, peppered with pine trees and Douglas firs. It had taken Sahana and James a little over an hour to drive out to it from downtown Seattle. They'd stopped by Pacino's to grab a quick bite along the way—a couple of veggie bowls with a side of chips and their homemade spicy salsa. It was a little after two in the afternoon with the sunlight, turning the skies bright blue with a few white freckles of clouds.

Driving up the pathway to the inn, Sahana couldn't help but admire the beauty of the place—how serene it felt, and how quiet. She instinctively rolled down her car windows to breathe in the warm air.

"Hey, my hair's going to blow into a mess," James protested.

"You'll be fine. Enjoy the view, will you?" she said with a laugh, looking out her window to watch a couple of blue jays dive into the trees. "Well, it's a stunning property, no doubt about that." She'd seen pictures of it of course, but she'd never actually visited the place before.

"I think I'm wearing the wrong shoes for this," James noted, as they drove past the apple orchards that adjoined the property.

"Very clever to have orchards on the property, too," Sahana added, looking past James's qualms. "Inns with apple orchards garner thirty-percent more honeymooners than inns without," she added, steering the car down the pathway.

"Did you just make up that metric?"

Sahana smiled. "I never make shit up...well, unless I'm in court representing a client," she added with a playful wink. "No, I read that somewhere. Plus, it's not just the honeymooners, right? Kids love to pick fruit...apples, blueberries, pumpkins? Not to mention orchards are great for a wedding venue. I think it's *very* clever."

James let out a sigh. "I feel like I'm on my way to Mr. Darcy's house. How long is this freakin' driveway?"

Sahana peered through her windshield. "There, right up ahead," she said, her eyes coming to rest on the magnificent Tudor-style inn, with the driveway circling before it, around the lush green front lawn, with cushion-like flower beds and trimmed box hedges.

"On second thought, maybe I did pick the right shoes," James said, as he considered the place.

The inn wasn't overly expansive but very elegant looking. Pulling her Mercedes around the full length of the circular drive, Sahana pulled to a stop in one of the open spots on the pebbled parking lot that aligned the front lawns. She stepped out of her car, with James following suit. She did her best to navigate her way across the loose pebbles, as her Jimmy Choos caught in them, tipping her off-balance on more than one occasion. "I think you might be right about the shoes," she said with a grunt, when they finally made it to the front door of the inn. Taking her shoes off one at a time, Sahana emptied them of the tiny pebbles that had managed to hitchhike a ride.

Slipping them back on, she straightened out her tweed skirt and turned to James. "How do I look?"

"Hot," he replied casually, straightening his own bow tie.

"James?" Sahana shook her head. "Not the truth. Tell me what I want to hear, please."

He sighed. "You look like a future junior partner at Yoland and Wiseman."

Sahana breathed in. "Good. Yes. That's exactly right." Turning, she walked in through the open door.

IT WAS A stunningly decorated foyer. Perhaps one of the best Sahana had ever seen—an eclectic design that sported a mix of wood paneled ceilings, darker-colored accent walls that were complemented by colorful, floral rugs, tapestry, and furniture. A beautiful hummingbird-patterned wallpaper, vintage tables, and paintings and art photos along the walls. To Sahana's left, the foyer appeared to open out to a quiet reading room, to her right was a beautiful common room that captured the best of the day's natural light. A few people, who Sahana assumed were inn guests, walked through the foyer, which boasted a large stairway that she imagined led up to the guest rooms. And straight ahead, was a reception desk with a beautiful antique lamp, a couple of flowerpots, and a computer. Behind the desk, stood a young woman with curly blonde hair that fell down to her shoulders. She appeared to be in her early twenties, with lively hazel eyes and a sprinkle of freckles across the bridge of her nose. She wore jeans, a flannel shirt, and riding boots.

"Hello," she said, with a welcoming smile. "Are you folks checking in?"

"Hi, no, not checking in," Sahana replied, stepping forward to hand the woman a business card. "I'm Sahana Sood, and this is my assistant, James Ware. We work at Yoland and Wiseman and we're looking to speak to either Clive or Sigi Harring, who run this establishment…or both?" she added with a dry chuckle.

"Oh, I'm sorry they're both visiting a vendor. But if you like you can leave a message for them or you're welcome to wait, although I'm not sure when they're due back," she said, gesturing to the adjoining lounge area. "I'm Holly, by the way, their niece. I'm just interning here this summer."

"Niece?" Sahana repeated, exchanging a quick look with James.

"Niece," he confirmed.

Sahana extended her hand out. "Very nice to meet you."

They shook hands, following which Sahana ruefully considered her options. Neither one sounded appealing. She didn't have time to sit around waiting for Clive and Sigi, and she didn't think leaving a message would yield a response. She needed face time with these people. "Well, we're here on business relating to the inn," she explained. "Is there anyone else we can talk to who's directly involved in the running of it?"

Holly frowned. "Oh, I think the best person for that would be my cousin, Ryan Mehra. He owns the place."

"Yes, we've been trying hard to reach him," Sahana said, dryly. "Your cousin never picks up his phone or returns calls."

Holly laughed. "Yeah, he's his own boss like that."

"I thought you were boss, boss?" James whispered to Sahana, who shot him a frown.

"But you can just talk to him face-to-face, since you're here, anyway?" Holly added, causing Sahana to widen her eyes.

"Excuse me, what?" she blurted. "Talk to Ryan Meh—er, Mr. Mehra's *here*? At the inn? Right now?"

Holly paused for a moment, then shook her head. "Sorry, I should've mentioned that sooner. He'd been living in New York—"

"Right, right, right," Sahana said, urgently.

"But he came back about a week ago," Holly said.

"Where is he?" Sahana asked, as her eyes frantically darted across the rooms as if she were trying to find him herself.

"Oh, usually he's in the library, or maybe he's out walking. I can go look for you?" Holly said with a warm smile.

"Yes, could you? Would you?" Her heart was pounding.

"Sure, make yourselves comfortable and I'll send Ryan your way once I find him. You're welcome to walk around the property if you'd like."

Sahana smiled. "Thanks, I think we will," she said, grabbing James by the arm and leading him out the front door of the inn toward the gardens that surrounded it.

"Aow, aow, ao-w," he cried. "You're wrinkling the fabric on my shirt."

Stepping outside, Sahana turned to him, releasing her grip on his arm. "How did we not know he was back?"

"The man's been ghosting us, I doubt he was going to text us saying he was visiting Seattle, for God's sake," James replied, ruefully examining his sleeve.

"Okay-okay, you know what? It's fine. It's *fine*," Sahana said, between deep belly-breaths. "We didn't know it, but he's here. This is our chance—possibly our best and last chance, to try and rehook his interest in the acquisition." Her eyes involuntarily darted across the side lawns over to the slightly overgrown vegetation that bordered the inn. She peered in the distance, and for a second her eyes caught sight of a figure looming amidst the weeds and brush a few feet away from the parking lot. "Who's that?" she asked, squinting against the sunrays before pulling a pair of Ferragamo sunglasses out of her bag to slip on.

James looked up and squinted in the same direction as Sahana. "I don't know. Workmen? The gardener, maybe?"

"Come on, maybe he knows where Ryan is," Sahana said, beginning to walk toward the figure, her heels sinking into the soft grass with each step.

As they approached, she got a close-up look at the figure—a tall, broad-shouldered man with dark hair. His facial features mostly lay hidden under the shadows of the trees that surrounded the patch of brush he was hacking down with his large sickle blade. He wore whitewash jeans. *Just* whitewash jeans, and nothing else. Sahana noticed he had one hand raised upward to the sky. Streaks of dark red trickled down his raised hand like streaks of—

"God, is that blood?" Sahana gagged.

"I don't know, I haven't noticed the blood-part yet," James replied dreamily.

Sahana turned to him, only to catch him blushing spectacularly as he continued to ogle the topless gardener. "Will you please be professional? And remind yourself you're married?"

James let out a sigh. "I might be married, honey, but I'm still human," he said as they walked closer to the gardener in the brush.

They now stood just a few feet shy of the man. "Er, excuse me, sir?" Sahana said, trying to wipe the muck off the heels of her Jimmy Choos onto the grass. When she looked up again, she saw the man had paused his sickle-action and turned to face her and James, offering them both a full-frontal view of his ripped upper bod, complete, with a remarkable set of six-pack abs that glinted under the afternoon sun. His vanilla-white skin appeared sun-kissed, contrasting the dark hair on his head. He had that classic, Vogue-model jawline, made pretty by stubble—the kind of annoying distraction that could trip up an otherwise professional, female corporate attorney on her way to a junior partnership. His sculpted features appeared to soften under his hazel eyes and thin lips that curved at either end.

James let out a gasp, which Sahana quelled with a hard frown.

"Sir, do you know where I can find Mr. Mehra?" she asked the man.

He walked toward her, sickle in one hand, a deep-set frown on his brow, his injured hand still raised up to the sky. Sahana could now confirm he was bleeding profusely. She cringed. "Er, you've got a little cut thingy, there," she said, vaguely pointing to his bleeding hand.

The gardener inched closer, decidedly making his way through the few remaining patches of weeds between them. He was headed straight toward Sahana.

"Would you like a Band-Aid?" she added, slipping a hand into her bag, trying to locate her travel-size, emergency first aid kit. The man now stood before her, in all his sweat-blood glory, and with James hyperventilating beside her.

"What do you need Mr. Mehra for?" he asked. His voice was deep and warm. His frown hadn't budged an inch.

"It's business related," Sahana replied, with a calm nod. Her desire was evenly split between wanting to check the state of the man's bloody hand, and admiring his perfect five-o'clock-shadow.

"Mr. Mehra's busy just now," the gardener replied. He

began turning away.

"This is important," Sahana said, catching him in his tracks. "Do you at least know where he is?"

The man turned again. "I know his *exact* location," he replied, his face looking directly down into hers. She felt their gazes collide, through the tinted lenses of her sunglasses. "And I'd be happy to point you to it, if you tell me what it's about."

Unbelievable. Sahana felt her jaw drop open with disbelief. She turned to James for assistance. "Could you j-just...please reason with the farmer?"

"Gardener," James amended, clearing his throat. But before he could say another word, Sahana dove back into the boxing ring.

"Look, pal, we don't have time to play games here, alright?" she said, lifting her sunglasses up above her head, her brown eyes directly meeting her oppressor's piercing hazel stare for the very first time. The moment felt like a pause, as they took each other in. She could smell his scent—spicy cologne, with a hint of blood, a whiff of the outdoors, and a whole lot of nerve. The two of them remained locked in a staring contest, with Sahana refusing to concede, and the gardener refusing to comply. Her heels were sinking into the grass, however, and her neck hurt from staring up into his face because he was so damn tall. But no way was she going to let this topless, bushwhacker with his steamy good looks get in the way of her professional agenda.

"You don't want to tell me where your boss is, fine," she finally said. "I'll find him myself. In fact, I prefer it that way, because when I do find him, I'm going to report you to him."

"*Report* me?" the man asked, licking his lips combatively.

"That's right," Sahana said, determined to appear unfazed, at least outwardly. "I'm going to tell him you were in violation of sanitary codes pertaining to…i-insufficient clothing, improper hygiene, and—"

"Ryan, there you are!" called a voice from behind them, cutting Sahana short. She turned to catch Holly running toward them. "These folks are here to meet you. They're from Yoland and Wiseman. Oh, but looks like you've met already?"

Sahana felt her blood turn cold as she and James exchanged a fleeting glace before turning back to the man who she now realized was no gardener, but Ryan Mehra in the flesh, with *tons* of blood.

Holly paused when she caught sight of Ryan's bleeding hand. "Don't tell me you cut yourself again? I told you, Uncle Clive can clear the brushes when he gets back."

"It's a scratch. I'm fine," Ryan said, keeping his gaze firmly on Sahana. "Did you say Yoland and Wiseman?"

"Sahana Sood," Sahana said. She extended her hand out to him. "A pleasure to finally meet you, Mr. Mehra." He'd gone from underdog to top dog in five seconds. And just when she expected he'd snub her handshake as punishment for the misguided threats she'd made to him, he switched his cutting tool over to his bloodied hand before reaching his unbloodied one out to return the shake. They locked eyes. His grasp—his skin, felt warm against hers. She gently retracted her hand, unsure of why her heart was beating so fast.

"Hi, I'm James Ware," James added, quickly reaching to shake Ryan's hand, also.

"You know, I'd love to stay and chat," Holly cut in. "But I need to get back to the reception desk."

"Thanks, Holly," Ryan said, throwing her a smile as she turned and headed back to the inn. He turned his attention right back over to Sahana.

It was her cue. She cleared her throat. "Mr. Mehra, I hope you'll overlook our er, earlier er—"

"Yes?" Ryan nudged.

The twinkle in his eyes didn't escape her. "Misunderstanding," she decided.

To her relief, he nodded. "No problem," he said, as he began walking past her and James toward the inn.

"Wait, Mr. Mehra, we need to talk," Sahana said, watching as Ryan now walked over to the side of the inn. Placing his gardening tool down, he pulled a T-shirt out of a toolbox to slip on.

"Talk about what?" he asked, continuing to rummage in the toolbox. "Thought I had a first aid kit in here," he mumbled to himself.

"Oh, please, Mr. Mehra, allow me," Sahana said quickly. Reaching into her bag, she pulled out a travel-size first aid kit and stepped closer to him to take a brief look at the cut on his palm. It wasn't bleeding anymore. "I want to talk to you about the acquisition," she said, unzipping the kit to pull out a large adhesive bandage, which she handed to him.

He accepted it. "Thank you." He peeled the backing off before taping up his wound. He started to walk off, then stopped. "Look, I thought I made it clear? I don't want to sell my property. Not anymore."

Sahana tiptoed behind him, trying to keep her heels from sinking into the grass. James walked alongside her. "Yes, I understand you communicated a change of heart, but—" Sahana paused to look down. They were off the grass now, and on the cobbled driveway. She noticed her shoes. The bottom inch of it and her heels were all muddy. She looked back up at Ryan. "Could you excuse me one moment?" she said. Turning, she strutted back over to her car a few feet away. She opened her trunk and from it she pulled out a clean new pair of Gucci pumps which she slipped on in place of the muddy ones. She neatly placed the dirty shoes in a brown paper bag before closing her trunk and walking back to Ryan, aware of his eyes on her the entire time.

"Sorry about that," she said, returning to meet a curious smile that had cropped up on his face.

He nodded as if with approval. "Never seen that technique before. Did they teach you that at your fancy law school?"

This guy was a pill, Sahana decided. *Perfect. I can swallow him whole.* "Actually Mr. Mehra—"

"Ryan," he insisted.

"Ryan," Sahana continued, "you'll be happy to know, you and I both went to the same school."

He paused. "Don't remember seeing you around. And I got around a *lot*."

She glared back at him, her eyes flickering with an undetectable hint of sarcasm. "Must've been nice to get around so much," she said. *Schmuck.*

He exuded a handsome laugh. He'd caught the hint. "I

didn't mean *around*-around. I just meant—"

"Please, Ryan," Sahana said waving the flat of her palm at him. "You don't need to explain. In fact, the primary reason for my coming here is to understand what prompted you to change your mind about the acquisition."

He pursed his lips. "I guess I decided it was in my best interest, long-term, to retain ownership of the place."

"Fair enough," Sahana acknowledged. It was something she'd learned early on in her career as an attorney—sometimes the best way to win an argument is by pretending to concede the point. "But you live and work in New York and your aunt and uncle are nearing retirement age, as you mentioned to me when we first spoke. And you said you have a mortgage on the property. Wouldn't it be more prudent for you from a long-term perspective, to consider selling? And acquisition will take the pressure off of you having to manage the place, you can pay off your loan, and still have enough left over from the profit for you to maybe even consider buying a place on the East Coast—Cape Cod, maybe, or Maine?"

Ryan's gaze narrowed. "I have money put away and the inn's pulling in good revenue. I'm sure I'll find a way around the loan. And I intend to run the inn when my aunt and uncle retire which should be easy to do now, because I don't live in New York anymore. I moved back here for good a few weeks ago."

Sahana grimly absorbed this new information. "I see." This was bad, bad, bad. If he'd moved cities and mapped out a twenty-year plan, then there was a bigger reason in play behind Ryan's decision not to sell, than she'd thought.

Which inevitably pointed to a slimmer chance of him changing his mind.

The look on her face appeared to please him and he smiled. "I think I've answered your question," he said, conclusively.

"You know what, you have," Sahana said. "And I appreciate your time and I completely respect your decision. But if for some reason you change your mind," she said, reaching in her bag and pulling out a business card which she extended to him. "I hope you'll get in touch."

His gaze remained steady on her, and hers on him. He accepted the card. "I'm sorry you had wasted a trip," he said.

But he didn't look sorry. In fact, Sahana watched as a smile threatened to break free around the corners of his lips. She smiled back, as if boldly unaffected. "On the contrary. It was eye-opening."

Chapter Four

"WHAT NOW?" JAMES asked Sahana as they sat back in the car.

She began pulling her car out of the pebbled driveway of The Wildling Inn. Her gaze drifted to the porch, where Ryan Mehra stood with his arms firmly crossed against his broad chest. He watched her with a smile, smug as ever, as she drove around the circular drive, right past him. Driving out the inn's open gates, Sahana caught one last image of him in her rearview mirror. He hadn't budged an inch. He likely wasn't even blinking.

She tore her gaze away from the rearview mirror as they drove away, up the broader road ahead. "Now? Nothing," she declared. "Clearly, Ryan's not about to take the money and ride Old Thunder off into the sunset. But it doesn't mean we give up. We can't force him to sell if he doesn't want to, James. What we can do, is follow up with him a few months from now and try our luck again. Give him time to cool off."

"He seems pretty headstrong. You're like a match made in heaven," James said, ruefully. "What about your promotion? You said this could impact it?"

"I'm worried it could. But I'm hoping it won't." The

words felt dry on Sahana's tongue.

"I'm sure the board will be fair in its decision," James said, reassuringly.

"I'm sure," Sahana replied, shy of being convinced.

The light in the sky was beginning to fade with the setting sun. By the time Sahana pulled into the underground driveway of her downtown office, it was close to six o'clock.

James stepped out of the car, and turned to her while she stayed seated behind the wheel, engines purring. "Are you coming back up?" he asked.

Sahana shook her head. "No, I promised my mom I'd drop in to check on a cousin tonight."

"Okay. And no next steps with Ryan Mehra for now?" he asked again.

Sahana nodded. "None."

BEFORE SAHANA BEGAN her drive to Bellevue where Shaan and Misha lived, she sent her mother a text. *"On my way to see Shaan and Misha."*

Her mother's reply was instant. *"Good. Remind him of our Rakhi celebration this weekend."*

Sahana sighed, turning her car into the street. Maybe someday she'd figure out why she so desperately needed to please her mother. But until then, she resigned herself to staying caught in the woman's web of expectations—the burden of living up to them day in and day out.

Driving down to Bellevue, Sahana made a quick stop at Palazzo's Pizza to pick up a large veggie pizza, with everything on it and headed straight to Shaan's. When she arrived, she pulled into the driveway outside his condo and stepped out of her car to study the place. It appeared to be a quiet, residential neighborhood with pretty pink sidewalk flowers and well-maintained lawns outside each home. It was so unlike Shaan. The man was a writer, and as far as Sahana could remember, he'd never gone for cookie-cutter anything. He'd been a pre-med student who'd ended up switching majors in college because he was convinced writing was his calling. He'd fallen hard for an exchange student from India, Anita Darr, whom he'd married and followed back to India, despite his parents' plea for caution. They'd never been sold on Anita's whimsical personality. Sahana's mother had joined the bandwagon along with them, vehemently opposing the match. "Anyone who claims they have a crush on Lord Shiva is not a wife-type," Sharmila had said to Shaan once. But he was sure his love for Anita, and hers for him, was real. *So* sure.

Sahana carried her warm pizza up the boxwood-lined walkway. She checked her watch. It was eight thirty, but the lights inside the condo appeared to be turned on, so she registered a gentle knock on the door instead of ringing the doorbell, expecting Misha would be asleep.

The last time she'd seen Shaan was three years ago, when he and Anita had visited them. Anita had an art gallery showing in Boston. They'd both flown into Seattle to spend time with his parents for a few days before heading back to India. Rumors had already begun circulating, however, of tensions in their marriage. A few family gatherings had even witnessed heated arguments between them, which had surprised everyone including Sahana, considering Shaan was known to be a calm, easygoing personality who rarely ever put his emotions on display. And now, with him and Misha back in Seattle, and no mention of Anita, the aunties in the family had begun churning up rumors again about a major development. Something had to have happened between Shaan and Anita. Which is why Sahana knew her mother wanted her to visit him—so she could uncover the truth, bring it back to her mother like the faithful golden retriever she was. Sahana knew her mother was very close to Shaan's parents, who lived in the same lakeside neighborhood as them. Any information her mother could gain about Shaan and Misha would be widely received by Shaan's parents, and widely believed, since it was coming from the noble source that was Sharmila Sood.

When the front door opened, Sahana gasped as her eyes met Shaan's for the first time in years. "Oh my God, Shaan..." She felt the words slip out of her lips before she could filter them. Shaan, neck down, looked as handsome as she'd remembered him, from three years ago. He was tall and athletic. He'd always been athletic. He'd run track in high school, played soccer all through college, and had been devoted to bike racing for over a decade. His body appeared unchanged to her, as she studied him in his black tee and relax-fit jeans. But neck up, Shaan had changed. He'd grown a full beard, from out of nowhere, apparently. She'd never ever remembered him slacking on a shave. His otherwise handsome, deep-set eyes appeared tired. But when he smiled at her, he looked a little like the man she remembered.

"Hey, Sahana," he said, extending his arms out to give

her a hug, which she returned with earnestness.

"It's been so long since I saw you. You've changed…or a good part of you has," she said, as he led her into his home. The place looked small but clean. Knowing Shaan, Sahana expected no less. He was always such a perfectionist, which is exactly why she got along so well with him, out of all her cousins. "Where's Misha? Asleep?" she asked.

He nodded. "She was pretty whipped, waiting for Anita to call and, well, she basically fell asleep, waiting, so…" His voice trailed off, as did his gaze, toward the kitchen. "Do you want a beer?" he asked her.

She nodded. "I'd love one, thanks. And I got us a pizza with everything on it," she said, trying to inject some hope into the seemingly heavy air in the room.

"Great," Shaan replied, almost tiredly, heading into the kitchen to grab a couple of beers.

Sahana slipped her high heels off, and shed her tweed jacket on the couch. She placed the pizza on the coffee table and sat down on the rug beside it, with her legs neatly tucked under her.

Shaan returned with two beers, two plates, and two napkins.

"Perfect," Sahana said with a smile as she reached her hand up to accept one of each item. God, she'd missed him. She only realized it now, when she was exposed to how compatible she and Shaan were, and always had been. She watched as he sat down on the rug next to her and raised his bottle up to hers.

"Cheers," he said with a soft smile that didn't quite make it to his eyes. "To good old times."

Sahana smiled back and clinked her bottle to his. "Best years of our life, wouldn't you say?" she asked him.

He sipped from his bottle, opening the pizza box to tear out a slice. "Yup."

Sahana was ravenous, too, so she reached over to grab a slice for herself. The melted flavor of cheese combined with the herb-laced marinara sauce sent a warm feeling through her, granting her permission to speak again. "So, how are you? I feel like you've been so quiet since you and Misha got back from India," she said.

Shaan kept his eyes on the pizza slice as he picked up a napkin to wipe the sides of his mouth. He shrugged. "I didn't have a whole lot to report, I guess."

"But you still haven't told any of us why you're back so suddenly? And Misha's here with you? At first we thought you were visiting, but your parents seem to think you're back for good and it appears you're renting a condo? And you bought a car?" Sahana paused to consider her cousin with a soft frown. He still wasn't looking at her, and continued to eat his pizza in silence, wiping his mouth at regular intervals. "Shaan? Seriously, what's going on with you? You can tell me, you know."

When he turned to her, she could see the overcast look in his eyes. "No, Misha and I aren't visiting. We're here to stay."

Sahana watched him with worry. And boy, did she have questions for him. But she knew Shaan. He'd confide in his own time, and he'd speak only if he had something to say. She loved that about him. And the last thing she wanted was to bombard him with questions when life was clearly mistreating him. She nodded. "I just wanted to make sure you're okay."

"I'm not," he replied. "But Misha's my priority, and she's not in a great place right now with everything that's happening..." Shaan appeared to trail off again as he picked up his beer to drink.

Sahana reached out to rub his back. This was hard to watch. She wanted to ask him what happened, but she couldn't bring herself to do it. Something had gone down, and it had taken Shaan along with it.

"Enough about me, how're you?" he asked, turning to her. "Are you still blazing a trail in the Sood family with your high-flying career?"

Sahana smiled at him at the same time her heart sank. "Oh, I'm blazing trails, alright," she admitted. "But for all the wrong reasons."

Shaan nodded as if he understood. He reached for his beer and drew another long sip. "You mean your marital status is upsetting Punjabi moms everywhere?"

"No, not everywhere. Just in the Lake Sammamish area. Just in the Sood household," Sahana said dryly. She picked her beer up to drink, feeling its airiness on her lips as it traveled down her throat, calming her nerves along the way. "Mom keeps setting me up with weirdos and I keep turning them down. And every time I reject a potential match, I feel like I'm pulling a brick out of Mom's happiness, not to mention she hates the idea of me freezing my eggs—"

Shaan coughed up his beer. "Your *what*?" he asked, looking bemused.

Sahana shrugged back. "Well, I'm not getting any

younger. At least that's what I hear at every family gathering, from every auntie I ever speak to, not to mention my OB-GYN. And honestly, I can't seem to find the right man. And it's not like I'm not trying, Shaan, I am."

"I know," he said with a warm smile. "I bear witness to that fact. And I remember how in high school you made your then-boyfriend, Varun Bose, sign that contract saying he'll marry you once he finds a job."

This caused her to laugh. "Oh God, I was such an idiot. I'd never marry Varun now," she said.

"So, whatever happened to him? Did he become a doctor in the end? Made his parents proud?" Shaan asked.

"Varun? Oh, he hit the bullseye pretty close. He's a professor of Economics at the University of Washington, so *technically*, he's a doctor," Sahana said. "And he completely made up for any shortcomings by marrying Rani Kumar and giving his parents three grandkids."

"Three, huh?" Shaan asked with a raised brow.

Sahana shrugged. "Well, if he'd become a *real* doctor he could've gotten away with just two kids, but he botched that. So, yeah, three."

"Wow." Shaan let out a soft laugh, which allowed her to admire the handsomeness of his smile even through the thicket of his new, condolence-beard.

"Anyway," she said, trying to distract herself from the itch of wanting to uncover the reason behind Shaan's woes. "I told Mom at yoga the other day that I'm thinking of freezing my eggs, because I really am. If I can't find a husband, I at least want kids."

"And how did Mummyji take it?" Shaan asked with a

devious smile. He, along with all of Sahana's cousins, referred to her mother as *Mummyji* and her father as *Papaji*.

"Extremely well." Sahana nodded with sarcasm. "I mean I was expecting she'd get up and rip my yoga mat in half, but she didn't. She just growled, called my plan a bullshit idea, and threatened to set me up with four more men, out of which she's sure one is my Mr. Right. Or, at least, Mr. Satisfactory. So yeah, overall, great result to that conversation." Sahana reached for more pizza. The story of her life sounded pathetic even to her. She couldn't hear herself talk about it anymore.

"Aunties will always be aunties, you know that," Shaan said.

"Yeah, I know," Sahana said. "But it's not helping my case that all our cousins are married. I mean, even *Laila* got hitched."

"Oh yeah, I heard about that. Mom wanted me to come to the wedding, but I, er, had a lot going on," Shaan said. "Didn't she marry a doctor?"

Sahana rolled her eyes. "Yup. Dr. Hari Singh. The bitch stole the only guy who came close to Mr. Right."

Shaan laughed. "No, not again?"

Sahana joined his laugh. "But Hari and she are madly in love. So, he wasn't made for me, anyway. Isn't that what Dadima used to tell us when we were kids? If you didn't get it, it wasn't made for you?"

"Yup," he said with a nod. "Although, I still think you've got a lot going for you, Sahana. I mean look at you, you're a successful female attorney, and aren't you in line for that promotion at your firm? The one you told me about when we chatted on the phone a few weeks ago?"

Sahana's spirit cramped. *Oh God.* "Yeah, that…" She swallowed hard. "Turns out, I might be running against luck there, too."

Shaan frowned. "Why, what do you mean?"

Breathing in, Sahana gulped down the last of her beer. "I mean, I'm in a good place, and I've done well at the firm. But there are things beyond my control that could potentially jeopardize my promotion."

"Or maybe it won't," Shaan said with a wink.

Sahana loved that about him. His willingness to pump life into something even as he was running out of air himself. "I guess I'll have to wait and see."

Shaan's phone rang at that very moment. He reached over to pick it up, pausing to look at Sahana. "I've got to take this one."

"Oh, go right ahead," she said, with a wave of her hand.

Shaan rose up from his seat as he answered the call. She watched as he walked over to the kitchen a few feet away, where she could still hear him talking to the caller. "Hey. No, she's asleep. What were you expecting?" He seemed to pause to listen for a moment before speaking again. "She did wait for you, Anita. She waited and waited, and fell asleep waiting for her mom to call. You told her you'd call, and you didn't. Why do you always make promises you can't keep?"

Sahana, who was well within the eavesdropping zone, cringed inwardly. She pulled her phone out of her purse, pretending to be busy on it. But she could hear enough and more as Shaan continued to talk.

"I don't care, alright? I don't care about any of your reasons or excuses. If you can't keep your promises to Misha, don't make them. No, I won't tell her you called, because that's just going to upset her." Shaan paused again. "You know what, I'm done. I've got company here. I gotta go. Bye."

Sahana turned away just as Shaan marched back to his seat on the rug. She could see, plain as day, the rage in his eyes. He was breathing fast, and he was staring blankly at the phone in his hand. "You okay?" Sahana asked him.

Shaan stayed silent, but just when Sahana decided he wasn't going to speak, he did. "We're getting a divorce, Anita and I. It's why I'm back here with Misha."

"I'm so sorry, Shaan," Sahana said slowly. She'd guessed it. And now, he'd confirmed it. "I'm sure it's been hard on you and Misha."

Shaan coughed up a dry laugh. "Yeah, it's been nothing short of a nightmare for Misha. But the sad truth is our divorce is the high point in our marriage."

Sahana frowned. "What do you mean?"

Shaan shook his head. "I just...I don't want to talk about it. But the papers have been signed and we got married in India, so my lawyer there's working to tie up any remaining loose ends. So, we can make it official."

"What about child custody? The courts tend to favor the mother, so if you need any help finding a good lawyer to fight your corner, I may have some contacts in India."

Shaan let out a soft chuckle. "No contest," he retorted. "And I couldn't be more grateful. Anita doesn't want Misha."

The words felt heavy as he dropped them, one by one.

Sahana felt completely inadequate as she reached her hand out to squeeze his arm. "God, I'm so sorry, Shaan."

"Well, shit happens. But I've got a friend who's been helping me. He and I went to college together. I don't think you've met him ever, but he moved out of state for a while and he's going through some life changes too, so he's back in Seattle now. He's been there for me. He helped me find the condo, and helped me move in, and…anyway, I'm not alone is what I'm saying. But I haven't told my parents about any of this yet, so—"

"I won't tell anyone, I promise." Naturally, Sahana, in an attempt to fetch information for her mother, had earned herself a bad reputation among her cousins for being a family gossip. But Shaan was different. He was an important person in her life. More important than her mother's accolades. "But you'll have to tell your parents at some point, Shaan. They'll find out, eventually, you know," she said.

"Yeah, I know."

"Maybe you and Misha should come to the Rakhi get together at Mom's house. She wanted me to tell you."

"I don't know, Sahana. I don't want to throw myself to the wolves yet." Shaan shook his head.

"Come on, they may be wolves, but they're still family. And what about Misha? Don't you think exposing her to some family comfort would help, instead of isolating her this way in the midst of a family crisis?" she asked him.

He appeared thoughtful, as he massaged his temple. "I know what you mean, I just—I can't face our crazy relatives right now." He turned to her. "I'm guessing you're going?"

"Are you kidding? If I don't go, Mom will set fire to my

condo in the middle of the night, so I'll be forced to move in with her permanently," Sahana said. *No, seriously.*

Shaan offered a weak smile. "I can totally believe that."

"So, will you come then? You'll get to meet all your cousins, and you know I always tie you a Rakhi each year, so if you're not there, I'll be forced to tie one on Dr. Hari Singh, my cousin's new husband whom I was supposed to marry. Can you picture the awkwardness?"

Shaan laughed. "Alright, I'll think about it."

"Good," Sahana said with a smile and checked her watch. "I'd better get going, I've got a long day at work tomorrow."

Chapter Five

SAHANA'S CLOCK RANG at five in the morning, as always. But she was wide awake on her laptop when it did, and she shushed it right at the first ring. She'd been up since two, researching Ryan Mehra. Of course, she knew a lot about him, already. And yes, he'd made it clear he wasn't going to sell his inn. She couldn't change that fact. But somehow, her last meeting with the man had stirred up her curiosity about him—his don't-touch-my-stuff vibe, his casual stubbornness. She could almost relate to it. She was so much like that herself. And under less pressure-packed, ambition-driven circumstances, maybe she would've even liked to get to know him better.

When she was convinced enough time had been spent on the elusive Mr. Mehra, Sahana shut her laptop. Pressing the flat of her palm into her neck she craned it backward to relieve some of the stress it had absorbed through the hours. She reached over to check her messages on her phone. Four text messages, all from her mother, awaited her. She opened the first one:

"This is Boy Number 1: Chatrapal Singh. He is 36. He has a beard, but he might shave it off for you. He is a dentist and has his own practice. He goes by Chip. If you like him, say yes, I will set up a meeting. Mohanji thinks he is very good."

Sahana sighed and opened the attached photo. "Oh, God..." she let out and texted her mom back: *"No way."*

She opened her second text: *"This is Boy Number 2: Purab Rai, 33. He is the CEO of his father's company, Night Owl Security. His mother is the chairwoman of the company, so a career woman like you. He also has a beard but it is just a goatee and it is new, so don't ask him about it. If you like him, say yes, I will set up a meeting. Mohanji thinks he is very good."*

Sahana frowned. This was beginning to sound rather templated. She opened the attached photo. *Hmm.* Purab Rai looked nice enough. He was sitting on a motorbike which appeared borrowed because he looked slightly uncomfortable on it. He wore sunglasses, and oh, there was that insufferable goatee. She hated it. But she couldn't very well text back a second *"no." Maybe the goatee will look better in person?* She texted: *"Yes."*

"God, give me strength," Sahana moaned, as she gingerly opened the third text from her mother: *"Boy Number 3 is Rahul Verma. He is 33, a gynecologist, so you will get a lifetime of free examinations, think of that. And also, very little chance of your vajayjay disappointing him because he would have seen the worst. Yes, he may have seen the best, also, so maybe yours will end up somewhere in the middle? If you like him, say yes and I will set up a meeting. Mohanji thinks he is very good."*

"You've got to be kidding me," Sahana muttered to herself. She opened the attached photo, tilting her head involuntarily as she studied the image of Rahul sitting in a chair, reading what appeared to be the "Bhagavad Gita." Sahana texted her mother back: *"Absolutely not. And please don't text me about my vajayjay."*

"God, I need a freakin' mojito," Sahana groaned, as she

braced herself for the fourth and final text from her mother: *"This is Boy Number 4. His name is Darsh Malhotra. He is also a lawyer like you, so you will have lots to talk about. He is 32 and he loves kids. I know because his mother told me. You don't have to text yes or no for him, because I have already spoken to his mother about you. I am not sure when, but hopefully I will set up a meeting for you both. Plus, Mohanji thinks he is very good."*

"What?" Sahana cried out, hurrying to open the attached photo. She felt her nerves calm down a bit when she looked at it, however. Darsh appeared pretty normal as he sat posing with a cup of coffee. Unusual, considering her mother usually liked to send her pictures of psycho nut jobs who Mohanji thought were *very good*. Maybe this wasn't as bad as she'd feared, Sahana thought.

She checked her watch. Six thirty A.M. She felt tired, even though her day was just beginning. She'd drunk two cups of coffee already, but she was craving a third. Hurdles aligned her path ahead in her personal life, and now in her work, with Walter Cruz threatening her promotion. Plus, with the Rakhi celebrations coming up that Saturday, her Sood-spinster survival skills were about to be tested.

Peeling her French linen sheets off, Sahana achingly stepped out of bed. Her head hurt; her stomach was cramping. The thought of seeing an army of relatives that weekend, without a red-herring topic in hand, and with her love life exposed, appeared to have triggered some unseasonal PMS in her.

Making her way over to her bathroom, she rested her palms on the cool surface of her marble vanity top and leaned in to inspect her reflection in the mirror. With her dark-brown eyes, her heart-shaped lips, her peachy, glowing skin, and flowing shoulder-length hair, she looked respectably attractive, even in her frazzled state. She was, at least technically, a successful attorney, with a successful career. And she had a nice life—fancy car, fancy condo in a fancy neighborhood. Now if only she could find a man to fit in her technically perfect puzzle. Someone to shush the pressure—someone to help her with her life's laundry load.

MAKING HER WAY into the office, Sahana mentally outlined her agenda for the day. She had a bunch of client calls to make, and a quick inspection of her calendar revealed some team meetings that had cropped up. Her inbox was overflowing with emails as it usually did when she opened it each morning. She decided to knock out the ones marked as "high-priority" first. She flagged some for James to respond to on her behalf. Somewhere between developing a pitch deck for a potential client, Sahana heard a knock on her door. She looked up as Candace made her way into the office. "Hey, you," she said with a smile. She was holding a tiny gift bag.

"Hey." Sahana smiled back before turning back to her screen to finish a sentence and hit Save Draft. She turned back to Candace.

"How're you doing?" she asked Sahana, walking up to sit in the chair across from her.

"Fine, thank you, why?"

Candace leaned in. "I heard about The Wildling Inn deal falling through."

"Oh." Sahana shook her head. "It did. But, you know, there will be other inns. There will be other acquisitions. In fact, I just closed the Fiber-Arnez deal this morning."

"The multi-million-dollar merger?" Candace's eyes widened. "Congratulations. Go you."

"Thanks." Sahana smiled. "So, what's in the bag?" she asked, tipping her chin at the tiny, shiny hot pink thing that had taken residence on her desk.

"Oh, when James told me about your meeting yesterday with Ryan and you know, how it went down, how you thought he was the farmer—"

"Gardener," Sahana gently corrected. An image of Ryan inevitably came to mind, and she smiled to herself.

"Anyway, I thought you needed a little picker-upper. So, I stopped by Blush Because."

"My favorite boutique cosmetic store?" Sahana smiled.

Candace nodded. "And you won't believe what I discovered. They now have this amazing thing they call Miss Moustache? It's this black goo you apply to your upper lip, you know, like a moustache, and exactly two minutes later, you wipe it off and, voila, it takes all that unwanted peach fuzz right off. So, I thought I should get you one." Candace paused. "Wait, that didn't come out right."

Sahana laughed. "It came out exactly right." She accepted the bag. Peeking inside she retrieved the tiny glass jar. She vaguely inspected the charcoal-colored cream inside. "Thank you," she said, standing up to give Candace a hug. They chatted a bit longer.

After she'd left, Sahana reopened her deck and studied it. She'd edited it twice now, but she wasn't happy with it yet.

It was good, but not perfect. It needed more work, and she needed more coffee. Sighing, she rotated her neck as her eyes came to rest on the tiny Miss Moustache jar. Reaching for it, she read the instructions on the back. It was exactly as Candace had said: "Apply product directly on upper lip, or even over makeup, as if you were painting on a moustache. Leave it on for no more than two minutes. Wipe clean with dry try tissue or cloth."

Sahana considered the jar. Her upper lip did need some tending, and she only had a dewy primer on that day. She looked up past her monitor. The office seemed quiet, with everyone tucked away in their cubicles. *What the heck.* She unsealed it to retrieve the product and drew a generous line with it across her upper lip. *Mmm.* It felt cool against her skin. She checked the time on her computer, so she knew when to wipe it off and returned to working on her deck. Somewhere in between, her phone rang in her office. "This is Sahana Sood."

"Are you sitting down?" It was James.

"Yes. Why?"

"Marissa just pinged me from the reception desk. You have a visitor," he said with urgency.

"Visitor? Who?" Sahana frowned, quickly opening up her calendar. "Nothing's on here, James. If it's not on my calendar, I'm not going to—"

"It's Ryan Mehra."

Sahana felt her heart stop. She tried to grasp the fact. Why was he here? She thought he'd made it pretty clear his intentions not to sell. *Could he have changed his mind?* She stood up. "Show him in."

Her heart was now beating wildly. Sitting back down, she took a deep breath in, channeling poise. She repositioned herself before her computer. When she looked up, she caught sight of Ryan through the glass as he walked toward her office, led by James. He turned to look in her direction, but she looked away just in time, pretending to type things on her keyboard with casual urgency while appearing perfectly unfazed.

A moment later, James administered a gentle knock on the glass door. Sahana pretended to look up. "Yes?"

James entered, followed by Ryan. Sahana stood up and smiled. "Mr. Meh—I mean, Ryan. Nice to see you again." Walking over, she reached to shake hands with him. He looked incredible. He *smelled* incredible. His stubble had vanished, replaced by a clean-shaven face which highlighted his deep-set eyes and thin lips, not to mention that jawline. He wore a classic but casual black crew-neck sweater and khaki pants.

But something seemed out of whack. Ryan appeared to be grappling with a smile. She turned to James, whose eyes were blank as if it had absorbed a shock. "Thank you, James," she said to him with a nod.

But he seemed reluctant to leave, staring at her the whole time as if he were trying to tell her something.

"James?" Sahana glared.

He sighed and left.

She now turned her attention back to Ryan. "Would you care to sit down?" she asked him, leading her to the chairs at her desk. She walked around to her seat.

"Thanks." He cleared his throat but didn't sit down yet.

"Er, you've got a little er—moustache thingy on your face," he said slowly.

The words turned her lips cold as she suddenly remembered, with crippling horror, the goo she'd slathered on—now well past the two-minute mark. She covered her mouth, shuffling to find a wipe, a tissue—anything.

"Oh, please, Miss Sood," Ryan said. "Allow me."

Looking up, she watched as he slipped his hand into the pocket of his khaki pants and retrieved a travel-size pack of tissues and handed it to her.

Sahana froze. This was beginning to feel like déjà vu. She knew this scene from somewhere. *Oh, that's right.* It was the same scene from the day before, except now, she and Ryan had switched roles. She breathed in, determined to remain poised. "Thank you," she said, graciously. Opening the pack, she pulled a tissue out and wiped Miss Moustache off. *Hmm.* She paused to consider the tissue. *The thing really works,* she admitted to herself. She tossed it in the trash and sat down. Ryan followed her lead, his smile now roamed freely.

"So, how can I help you today?" She smiled back. Her upper lip, though, felt like it was on fire.

"I wanted to come down to apologize," Ryan said in that deep, handsome voice of his.

"Apologize? For what?"

"After you left, I kept thinking about yo—er, our meeting and I felt like maybe I behaved badly. I tried to push your buttons a bit. If I did, I'm sorry. That wasn't my intention."

She felt herself flush. "It's no problem. And you didn't behave badly. We showed up uninvited at your inn, so I think we can call it even."

Ryan smiled. "And I'm also sorry about not returning yours and James's calls and emails about the acquisition. I shouldn't have given you guys the runaround when I changed my mind."

This wasn't exactly what she'd hoped to hear. But oddly, the words didn't disappoint. "It's fine. I've been given the runaround by clients before. I've got the stomach for it. It's part of my job," Sahana said, leaning back in her chair.

Ryan nodded. "Still, I was hoping you'd let me make it up to you by letting me buy you dinner this Saturday."

"Dinner?" she repeated.

"You pick the place. My treat," Ryan added cheerfully.

Sahana smiled. The offer sounded harmless enough, but there was one problem. The Sood Rakhi celebration was Saturday. "I would've liked that, Ryan. But I can't this Saturday. I've got a family thing."

He nodded, although for a second Sahana thought she detected a splash of disappointment in his eyes. Before she had a chance to study his expression, however, he rose from his seat. "I understand and I won't hold you up. I know you're busy," he said, pulling his wallet out and from it a business card which he handed to her. "But if for some reason you change your mind," he added, once again appearing to take his cue from their last meeting. "I hope you'll get in touch."

A smile bloomed on Sahana's face. Reaching her hand out, she accepted the card. "Thank you. I sure will."

FOLLOWING RYAN'S DEPARTURE, Sahana walked over to James's cubicle. He was on a call, which allowed her the chance to lean her weight against his desk to help calm her electrified nerves. When he'd wrapped up the call, he turned to Sahana. "Oh, no moustache?" He raised a brow.

Sahana rolled her eyes. "Candace gave it to me as a present, and I didn't know Ryan would show up."

"God, I didn't know how to react when I saw you," James said with a laugh. "So, what did Mr. Hotness want? Don't tell me he changed his mind about the acquisition?"

Sahana coughed up a laugh. "I doubt Ryan will ever change his mind about it, James."

"Um, what's with the negativity?" James asked, cocking his head to one side.

Sahana shrugged. "It's not negativity. It's just my impression, based on my interactions with him."

"Okay." James nodded. "So, what did he come for?"

Sahana bashfully brought an image of Ryan to mind. "He came to apologize."

James squinted suspiciously. "I feel like there's more."

Sahana shrugged. "And he wanted to make it up to me."

"Make it up to you?" James frowned. "How do you mean?"

"By taking me out to dinner."

"I knew it," James cried. "I knew something was up with you two."

"What? Give me a break." Sahana waved him off.

"No, I could tell there was this..." James massaged the air. "I don't know, this mystical, magical, invisible energy..."

"Easy there, Elsa."

"No, I'm telling you, there was something there, between you and Ryan." James paused. "So, where's he taking you?"

"Oh, I didn't accept."

"What?" he cried out. "Why not? You've been going on about not finding a man, now here comes the hottest, most dateable man you've ever met, who likes you, and you said no, thank you?"

"Now, hold the phone, he wasn't asking me out, it was an olive branch. And second, I couldn't accept because I've got a big family thing happening."

"Can't you move it?"

"No, I can't," Sahana said, shuddering to think how her mother would react if she were to call and cancel. "But still, I think it's a step in the right direction with Ryan," she added.

"A foot in the door?" James asked with a smile.

Sahana smiled, back. "Exactly."

Chapter Six

SAHANA'S PARENTS, SHARMILA and Vinod, lived on Lake Sammamish, in a beautiful, waterfront home. They'd moved into the place a few years after Sahana was born, so the house, for her, carried wonderful memories from her childhood. Her father, Vinod, had moved to America more than forty-five years ago. As the oldest of three brothers, he'd inherited the role—and the heavy lifting—of being the head of the Sood family when his father died.

Sahana had watched him work hard all his life, as he slowly made his way up the corporate ladder, taking night courses, working weekends, working after hours. He'd missed family holidays, birthdays, and even a few annual trips back to Punjab, India. But in the end, he triumphed in his professional life. He'd managed to secure his family financially, and even found a way to get green cards for all his nieces and extended family. Sahana adored him. They weren't close, exactly, but she loved him very much. She knew and appreciated all he'd done to give her this life—the childhood she'd had, an arguably comfortable one, compared to many of her cousins back in India. But despite her admiration for him, Sahana knew her dad hadn't accomplished this alone.

He couldn't have. The reason he could go off and be the best version of himself the world had ever seen, was because of her mother, Sharmila. Sahana had witnessed it, how her young mother, who'd been married at nineteen years old, had coped with holding down the fort with two young daughters under the age of six and a husband who was always away, and always working. She remembered how her mom had had dreams—she'd wanted to work, wanted to study. But she'd put her life on hold to be there for Sahana and her sister, Samira. Her mom would wake up every morning at five, make her kids and her husband the kind of Punjabi-Indian breakfast that could resuscitate a corpse—stuffed parathas, filled with curried potatoes, with dal, and side of yogurt or at least a homemade pickle, if nothing else. She'd walk her kids to school, every day, rain, or shine, because the parathas now needed to digest, or they'd get sleepy in class.

They'd sing songs on the way, play word games, or on many occasions, Sharmila would tell them a mythological story about an Indian prince who almost always ended up finding a princess to marry. She'd always been there for Sahana and her sister. She'd had expectations for them, sure. And they'd diligently lived up to it, Sahana more than Samira because she was older. Older children in the Sood household always carried a greater onus when it came to their parents' expectations. But maybe that was Sahana's reason for always doing what her mother expected her to do. Her mother was her weakest link.

STANDING BEFORE THE large carved front doors of her parents' Lake Sammamish home, Sahana turned to eye the long line of cars that went down the street. They belonged to the relatives who were waiting for her inside her parents' home, attending her mother's annual Rakhi celebration. Aunties, uncles, cousins, second cousins, and unrelated cousins whom she treated like cousins because their parents were close. Every single year, for as long as Sahana cared to remember, they'd all arrived, like clockwork, bang, on every Indian festival, from Diwali to Holi to, well, Rakhi. For the most part, Sahana didn't mind seeing them. She was, after all, a proud Indian-American with a boisterous extended family. That was who she was, it was where she came from—her roots. She loved her family, she loved daily gatherings, and traditional Indian festivities; the smell of samosas, and the boom-boom Bollywood beats. But the thing she hated, the one and only thing she wished she could remove from the Sood-family equation, was her celibacy. Because today, it was going to turn into a giant headache.

Unlocking the front door of her parents' home with her spare key, Sahana entered, only to be intercepted, right in the foyer, by a swarm of relatives on their way into the large living room.

"Sahana? How nice to see you," one of them, Meena Auntie, her mother's second cousin, said. She was shimmering in her sequined red sari and blouse, accented by chunky pieces of gold jewelry.

"Thank you, Auntie," Sahana replied, bending down to touch the older woman's feet to show respect the traditional way.

Meena Auntie turned to her husband, Arnav Uncle who wore a traditional kurta-pajama. "Doesn't she look beautiful?"

He briefly regarded Sahana in her pink sari and large gold hooped earrings and nodded. "Absolutely." Like he'd ever dare to contradict his wife of many decades. Sahana proceeded to touch his feet also and he blessed her.

Shefali Auntie, her mother's third cousin, nodded in agreement. She was also looking her finest, dressed in a lovely chiffon sari, embroidered blouse, and diamond earrings. "Now, all you need is a *dulha* to complete the look." Dulha, meaning *groom* a.k.a. the thing she'd been trying to secure for many years, and failed. Sahana produced a dry smile before bending down to touch Shefali Auntie's feet.

"Your mother told me you turned down that nice boy, what was his name? Nakul? Nikhil?" Meena Auntie frowned.

"Nihal," Sahana said, in a tired voice. "He was a PhD student. Meaning, he was technically unemployed."

"But once he finishes his degree, you'll be married to a professor, no? And little things like that shouldn't matter. The *big* things matter like, is he home-loving, does he respect his parents, does he visit the temple on Sundays…"

"Will he be a good father," Shefali Auntie pointed out.

"Oh, *very* important," Meena Auntie agreed, turning to her husband for confirmation.

Arnav Uncle's head bobbled from side to side. "Very important."

"Thank you, Auntie," Sahana smiled, painfully.

"Don't worry, you can keep it in mind for the next one

when you meet him on Monday," Shefali Auntie said.

Panic flooded Sahana's brain. This was all new information coming her way and she hadn't even gotten past the foyer yet. "I'm sorry, I'm meeting who? When?"

"Purab Rai whose papa owns Night Owl Security, of course," Meena Auntie said.

"I didn't know I was meeting Purab on Monday?" Sahana bleated.

"Such a cultured family, too. Plus, when he inherits the business, you can manage the accounts…see? Win-win," Shefali Auntie added.

Sahana frowned. "But I'm an attorney not an accountant."

"Ah, okay. But still, you will want to help with your husband's business, no?" Meena Auntie countered.

"I don't know. I haven't met Purab yet," Sahana said. *A few more minutes and they'll be planning my freakin baby shower.* "I think I'll go see my mom," she added, trying to inch her way into the house, past the Sood linebackers.

"Okay," Meena Auntie said, grabbing Sahana by the hands. "But the next time I visit this house, it should be for your engagement party. Now, you're thirty, Sahana—"

"Thirty-two," she corrected, softly.

"Thirty-*two*? Oh, it's enough of this career-woman business. We all know what a great accountant you are—"

"Attorney."

"Yes, you're very good and now we just want you to be married and start a family," Meena Auntie said. "See, we all did it."

Sahana sighed. "Yes, of course."

A MANTRA FOR MISS PERFECT

WHEN SAHANA FINALLY managed to enter the kitchen, infused with the smell of fried food, and curry, she found her mother standing there, surrounded by her first cousins, all dressed in traditional Indian clothing. There was her cousin, Mira, married to a handsome white American entrepreneur, Andy Fitzgerald, who was presently holding their daughter, Anya, while Mira housed bun number two in the oven; Sahana's cousin Laila was there, also. She was a rock star by profession, which was a bit outside of the Sood-box-of-expectations, and her arm was covered in rose vine tattoos which was practically forbidden, but none of that held water, because she was married to Dr. Hari Singh, a pediatrician; her sister Samira would've been present, but she was traveling in Europe with her husband, Rohit. Sahana's eyes then clamped on the figure she loved most out of them, Shaan, who hadn't seen her yet, but who stood next to Laila, chatting while Misha sat coloring with the other kids at a corner table. It was Sahana's mom who spotted her first. "Sahana? Why are you so late?" she cried, as the latter approached the group.

"I would've been here sooner, but I ran into..." She sighed. "Never mind, I'm here now," she said, as her mother herded her over to the group.

"Hi Sahana," Mira said, reaching over to give her cousin a hug.

Laila was next. "We thought you'd run away or something," she said, with a wink. "Shaan here kept looking over his shoulder for you."

"That's because Sahana forced me to come today and she wasn't even here when Misha and I arrived," Shaan protested, reaching a comforting arm out to hug Sahana. Shaan gave the best brotherly hugs.

"I'd never miss Rakhi if Shaan's here, no way," Sahana said. She turned to her mother. "Mom, listen, I need to talk to you. I heard from one of the aunties you've set me up with Purab Rai for Monday?"

Her mom's brow creased. "Yes, so?" The other cousins tried not to pay attention, but Sahana knew they were within earshot. They were likely judging, passing looks. She felt sick, so she switched places with Shaan to move closer to her mother.

"I can't meet Purab on Monday. I've got to work."

Her mom shrugged, looking unaffected. "Meet him after work."

"I can't, I really just have a lot going on right now, Mom."

"You texted *yes* to Purab," her mom said.

Sahana nodded, feeling helpless. "Yes, but—"

"So, now you have a dinner meeting with Purab. I will text you his number. You pick the place, and he will be there. I have already spoken to him, and he told me he loves all cuisines. But still, pick something closer to Indian food. Maybe Thai food? Or Mexican?"

Sahana closed her eyes. She'd lost the battle.

"So, how's work going for you, Sahana? Aren't you in line for that promotion?" Mira asked, gently running a hand across her new baby bump.

The question sounded wholly unappetizing. She

shrugged. "I-er, it's in the works. And I don't know when it'll happen." She meant *if*, but she didn't dare say it.

"You'll get there. These things happen when they're supposed to, you know," Laila said.

"Yeah." Sahana nodded. Her instincts begged her to run the opposite direction.

"Maybe it's time to focus on the more important things," her mom cut in. "Getting married and starting a family before it's too late."

Sahana shuffled her weight between her feet as the angst rose up inside her. "Should we get started?" she asked the group. "Since we're all here now?"

To her relief, her mother agreed. "Yes, let's get started."

᠆᠆᠆᠆

IT WAS HOW the Soods always did it, their annual Rakhi celebration at Sharmila's house. The sisters, both youngsters and aunties alike, lined up, side by side, all traditionally dressed in either saris or flowing *lehenga*-skirts. The boys were smartly dressed in kurta-pajamas, standing across from their respective sisters. The sisters held a decorated plate before them, containing a *diya* lamp, a bowl of vermilion and traditional Rakhi bracelets, made out of either glittery beads or fancy paper.

Each sister circled the tray with the lamp lit, three times in a clockwise direction before their brother or brother figure. They added a spot of vermilion to their brother's forehead, following which they tied a Rakhi—a traditional Indian bracelet, embellished with beads and colorful threads, onto their brother's right wrist. The brother would give his sister, or sister figure money as a thank you. The same process was repeated until all the sisters had covered all the brothers, so by the end of it, the men each had a bunch of Rakhi bracelets to show for, while the women had earned a comforting chunk of change, not to mention the continued loyalty of a handful of brothers.

Sahana tied her Rakhis on Shaan, Andy, Hari, and a bunch of other cousins. By the end of it, she was richer by many hundred dollars, because while she stank at finding a soul mate, she was incidentally, an *excellent* brother-magnet.

She walked over to sit by Misha, who was busy counting the dollars on her lap which she'd earned from the Rakhis she'd tied around the room to her little cousins. "Hey, kiddo," Sahana said, sitting down next to Misha on the couch.

The little girl looked up. "Sahana Bua!" she cried out and reached over to hug her.

The hug felt soothing, nonjudgmental, and Sahana relished it before Misha pulled away again.

"So? How much did you make?" she asked her niece.

"A *lot* of monies," Misha replied. She had beautiful dark, curly hair, and had inherited the perfect blend of her mother's distinctly edgy features and her father's striking good looks.

"That's awesome. How're you going to spend it all?"

Misha shook her head. "I'm going to save it. All I need is a little more monies and I'll have enough monies to buy a plane ticket to India, to go see Mama."

Sahana tried to hide her dismay. "I'm sure she'll love

that, kiddo."

"Misha?" Sahana's mom called out, catching them both off guard. "Come, you and the kids can start eating dinner before it gets too late."

Misha nodded and slid off the couch, handing her stash of cash to Sahana. "Will you keep it safe for me while I eat my dinner?"

"Absolutely," Sahana said, as Misha walked away, and Shaan began walking toward her with a smile.

"So, she's found an attorney to oversee her finances, huh?" he asked with a warm laugh.

Sahana smiled back. "She's got a lot to learn, your daughter. Trusting lawyers like that?"

Shaan laughed. "She dives right in with people. No safety net whatsoever."

"I'm glad you came today," Sahana said.

"You were right about doing it for Misha. She needs to be around family. People who love her," Shaan said. His phone rang at that very moment, so he pulled it out of his pocket. "Oh, this is my friend from college," he added, looking at the screen and swiping to answer the call. "Hey man, yeah, I'm at my aunt's house. No, I don't think so, not this time," he said, shaking his head. "Yeah, I know I'm in shape for the race, it's not that. It's just I don't feel comfortable leaving Misha with a babysitter right now. My parents have plans, I don't want to impose on my aunt and uncle." He listened for a bit before signing off the call. "Thanks, no, appreciate you telling me, man. Maybe next time? Yeah, bye." He tucked the phone back into his pocket, his eyes absently staring at the floor.

"What was that about?" Sahana asked him.

"That was my friend. The one I mentioned to you?"

Sahana recollected with a nod. "The guy you know from college who's been helping you?"

"Yeah. He was just telling me about a track race on Monday. He thinks I should go, and I've got a membership and I pre-registered for it a couple weeks ago, but I'm not going."

"Why not? You should, Shaan," Sahana insisted. "Listen I caught most of what you said about not wanting Misha to be with a sitter. But maybe I can watch her. What time's the race?"

Shaan shrugged thoughtfully. "Four thirty, I think? At the Mac Quint Velodrome."

Sahana's mind rushed to settle logistics. She had work that day, and a few late afternoon meetings. But they were internal, so nothing she couldn't have James move around. The only other glitch was her match date with Purab Rai. Sahana wondered if she could meet him after seven, someplace in Redmond, which incidentally housed tons of Thai food restaurants. "I'll do it," she said with a bright smile. "I'll watch Misha. In fact, she and I can watch you race, and once you're done with it, I'll head out to meet Purab."

Shaan appeared thoughtful. "I don't know, she's been really emotional since the divorce."

"She'll love that, Shaan," Sahana said. "She needs to see you happy, you know. Remind her you're happy and loving your life, and she will follow close behind."

A smile flickered on Shaan's lips. "I had no idea you were this philosophical."

Sahana tipped her head matter-of-factly. "Yes, I'm a fountain of wisdom...for everyone but myself."

Shaan's smile bloomed into a soft laugh. "Okay, I'll do it," he said with a nod. "Although I have to warn you, there will likely be some kind of intro camp prior to the race."

"Misha and I can get ice cream while you do that, and we'll be back to watch you in action."

"I can't believe you're willing to do that," Shaan said, his eyes softening.

"I wouldn't do it for just anyone, you know. Just my favorite cousin and my favorite niece," Sahana said, reaching to give Shaan a bear hug, which he returned with equal enthusiasm.

Chapter Seven

MONDAY MORNING, SAHANA was up at her usual hour. She showered, brushed, flossed, blow-dried her hair, and walked over to her closet, wrapped in her organic Mediterranean towel. She'd already pre-picked two outfits the night before to choose from, to wear to her match date with Purab Rai—a mauve pencil skirt, matching purple silk blouse and jacket, and a black sheath dress, which was arguably a tad bolder than the other one. She drummed her fingers on her lips, unsure of which one to choose. This was her first meeting with Purab Rai. What if he was extra traditional? She wondered if she should meter her feminism. Squinting back at the two outfits, Sahana reached for the black dress. She wanted to find a husband, yes. But she wanted to find happiness along with him. If Purab was the kind who'd disapprove of her power-dressing, she'd prefer to know about it sooner rather than later. The black dress was the perfect way to test the theory.

She pulled her shoulder-length hair into a tight high ponytail, which incidentally, tended to elevate the shine of her high cheekbones with the added shea butter concealer and nude gloss lipstick. She considered her reflection in the mirror. *Simple, yet sophisticated—perfect.*

Once in the office, Sahana plowed through her dashboard of action items. She wanted to wrap everything up and be out by three to avoid the nightmare office traffic on Seattle's 520 bridge.

"Gorgeous!" James cried out when he popped into her office and caught her standing by the printer.

"Thanks," Sahana said, smiling back. "I'm just about ready to leave to meet Shaan and Misha in Redmond."

James nodded and pulled his phone out of his back pocket. "Your mother texted me. She wanted me to remind you not to talk about the goatee, tonight." He looked up. "Do I want to know the backstory?"

Sahana lodged a fist in her hip and let out a long sigh. "She's set me up with a potential matrimony match. The guy has a goatee, I don't like goatees, and my mom's worried if I ask him about it, I'll be forced to freeze my eggs and she doesn't want microwaved grandkids."

James's eyes widened. "Wow."

"His name's Purab Rai," Sahana added with a shrug. "I'm meeting him right after I see Shaan and Misha."

"So, your cousin Shaan's back for good, then?"

Sahana nodded, walking back over to her desk. "Yeah, looks like it. I adore him, so I'm glad he's back. I just wish his circumstances were different."

James frowned. "How do you mean?"

"He's just going through some things in his personal life, and it's been really hard on him. But he's got this friend who's been helping him through it."

"A *girl* friend? A potential rebound?"

Sahana shook her head. "I believe it's a guy Shaan went

to college with. Clearly he's someone Shaan trusts, or he'd never have accepted the help. In fact, he's the one who encouraged him to race tonight, which I think is a great idea. He needs to distract himself a little. Do what he loves to do."

"Track racing at the velodrome?" James asked. "I dated a biker once. They're feisty."

Sahana laughed. Bending, she picked up her laptop bag to swing on her shoulder, and three gift bags—two small ones and one large one with little sparkly ponies printed on it.

"Aw, is the pony one for me?" he asked, pretending to reach his arms out for it.

"Not this time." Sahana smiled, walking toward him and the door. "This is for Misha. It's her favorite MeMe Princess doll."

James's jaw dropped open. "The one that sells for a hundred and fifty dollars apiece?"

"Hey, she's my favorite niece."

"And you're her fancy auntie, no doubt." James laughed. "What's in the other two bags?"

"Oh, I thought I'd be fun to give Shaan and his friend a tiny gift at the end of their race, win or lose."

James leaned in to inspect the bags. Reaching in, he pulled out a box of gourmet chocolates from one of them. "Very nice," he mused. "I'd tell you you're one of the best gift-givers I know, but I'm afraid you'll gloat."

Sahana laughed and began walking past James toward the door. "How about you wish me luck instead, for my match date with Purab?"

"Good luck," James said, giving Sahana a warm hug,

which she accepted wholeheartedly. "You probably won't believe me, but something tells me you're about to meet your soul mate tonight."

She nodded. "I'll believe it when I see it."

Chapter Eight

WITH HER GIFT bags resting safely on the floor of her Mercedes, Sahana veered through the narrow inner roads of Redmond's Moorhill Park, toward the velodrome.

The parking lot, when she arrived, was already up to its maximum capacity, although Sahana managed to pinch one of the two remaining spots. Briefly, she checked her reflection in the rearview mirror, retouched her lipstick and tightened her high ponytail before grabbing her three gift bags and her Chanel clutch. She clicked the trunk of her car open, and walking around the back, switched out her Gucci pumps for a pair of black Dior sneakers. She'd done some research on the Mac Quint Velodrome, studied a map of the place. There was grass. And this time, she intended to maintain an upper hand on it.

Gift bags in hand, she made her way across the parking lot, her shoes playing beautifully with the soft, grassy earth underneath. She'd lived in Washington all her life, but never visited the velodrome before. As she walked into the arena, she passed a table with three people sitting behind it, two women and a man who all appeared to be race coordinators. A cardboard box sat primly before them on the table with a sign next to it that read: MQ DONATIONS.

Sahana pointed to the box. "Excuse me, what's this for?"

"Oh, it's a donation box," the man said with a nod. He was wearing a youthful smile that accented his golden hair and blue eyes.

"Donations?" Sahana asked.

"You can watch the race for free," one of the two women, a tall, athletic brunette, explained. "However, we recommend making a donation, you know, to help us maintain the track and spread awareness about the track racing sport—"

"Ah, got it, got it, got it," Sahana said, with quick nods. Reaching into her purse, she pulled out a twenty. She half-tucked the bill into the tiny opening on the head of the box. "Thanks." She smiled at the three coordinators.

"Thank *you*," the woman returned a grateful smile as she helped the money into the box.

The sun was beginning to set on a pleasant evening, as Sahana made her way closer to the tracks. Crowds of onlookers were scattered across the lawns adjoining the racetracks, chatting, laughing, eating ice cream. Racers clutching their bikes, wearing their sponsored kits peppered the lawns. The track wasn't open to them yet, so they stood on the grass with their friends and family who'd come to watch. Shaan had texted Sahana just before she left work, asking to meet her by the track, and right next to a large sculpture of a man riding a track bike, which Sahana assumed was Mac Quint himself, when she walked up to it. A second later, she heard a familiar voice.

"Sahana Bua!" Misha cried, as she came running toward her, arms wide open.

Sahana bent her knees to capture Misha's glorious hug. It was the best feeling ever, hugging her niece. "Are you excited about Daddy racing today?" she asked her. From the corner of her eye she caught two approaching figures in the distance who were walking a couple of bikes along with them. She kept her gaze locked on Misha, however, expecting one of the approaching figures was Shaan and the other, his friend.

"Yes, but I'm nervous, too," Misha said. "Do you think he'll win?"

Sahana brushed the little girl's flying hair into place as the evening wind played with it. "You know, the only thing that matters in a race is that you do your best and I know your daddy will do his best today, so we're going to cheer him on, no matter what, okay?"

"Okay." Misha nodded. Her eyes gently dropped down to the gift bags Sahana was holding. "What's that?" she asked in a meek voice.

"This is a present for my favorite niece," Sahana said, pointing to the large bag.

"Oh, but that's me!" Misha cried, excitedly.

Sahana laughed, handing her the bag. She watched with a melting heart as Misha pulled the hand-carved wood box out with the doll encased in it, her eyes widening.

"It's my most favorite doll in the whole world, thank you, Bua!" she cried out. Reaching forward, she gave Sahana a big hug. "But Daddy said this doll was too expensive. He said I could maybe *maybe* get it as a birthday present." Misha paused to look up at her aunt. "Are you rich, Sahana Bua?" she asked, flat out.

Sahana shrugged. "Mmm, yeah."

Misha nodded, looking satisfied. "Is that one for Daddy?" She pointed to one of the two smaller bags.

"Yup."

"Why? He's not your favorite niece," Misha asked, clutching her present tight.

Sahana smiled. "No, but he's my favorite cousin. And this is a good-job kind of present, for him and his frien—" Her lips froze just shy of uttering the *d*, as her eyes clamped first on Shaan before coming to rest on his friend—the one he'd been raving about who'd gone to college with him and been there for him these past months.

"Ryan?" Sahana cried out, her heart jumping up to her throat.

His eyes too were wide with surprise. But he promptly overcame it to manage a handsome smile. "Hello, again," he said. He was wearing his race kit—helmet, a pair of metallic navy, skin-tight knee-length shorts, and matching tee with the names of sponsors printed across it in white lettering. His eyes now scanned her from head to toe, pausing briefly at her feet. He looked up and smiled. "Nice shoes."

"Thank you. I never make the same mistake twice." Sahana smiled back.

Ryan let out a soft laugh. Their gazes remained comfortably locked, although for a second, Sahana felt like his eyes dropped down to her lips before rising up again.

"I was going to introduce you, but it looks like you two know each other?" Shaan said, with a warm smile.

Sahana realized she'd been so distracted by Ryan she hadn't even given her cousin a hug. "Hey, Shaan." She embraced him and he hugged her back. He was wearing the exact same kit as Ryan, color coordinated and everything, which she assumed was intentional.

"Your cousin tried to convince me to sell my inn," Ryan said to Shaan. But his eyes stayed put on Sahana.

"Your friend gave me the runaround when he decided he didn't want to," she replied, returning every ounce of his twinkling gaze.

"I thought we got past that," Ryan countered.

"I thought we did, too," Sahana replied with a tilt of her head.

"Do you guys like each other or not, I can't tell?" Misha frowned.

"Great question, kiddo," Shaan added with a laugh.

Sahana found it hard to resist a smile as Ryan smiled back. "We don't *dis*like each other," she said.

"No, not at all," he confirmed.

Shaan nodded. "Well, I'm glad that's sorted out." His eyes now caught sight of the bag in Misha's hand. "Kiddo, what's that you're holding?"

"Bua gave it to me," she said, beaming.

"I see," Shaan said and turned to Sahana. "But a tad expensive, don't you think?"

"Yeah, but I hope you'll allow it?" she asked.

"Just this once," Shaan conceded with a warm smile. "Thank you."

"What about us? Do we get fancy presents, too?" Ryan asked, his eyes twinkling.

Sahana nodded primly. "You get a chocolate box."

"Huh." Ryan frowned, as if he were unimpressed.

"A *gourmet artisan* chocolate box," Sahana clarified.

Ryan shrugged. "Godiva?"

"La Maison Du Chocolat."

He shook his head. "Never heard of 'em."

A smile instinctively wanted to break free on her lips. But she overruled it with a mock frown. "Then maybe you don't want my chocolate box?"

"Oh, no, I want it," Ryan said, his gaze once again arresting hers. "I want your chocolate box."

Sahana felt herself flush, as his words sent a cool tingle down her spine. She clutched the gift bags tighter.

At that very moment, the event organizers made an announcement for the racers to assemble inside the velodrome.

"We should get going," Shaan said, and turned to Misha. "Stay by Sahana Bua, okay?" he said, bending low to give her a hug.

"Good luck, Daddy," Misha replied, dropping a warm kiss on his cheek.

Ryan watched them before turning to Sahana. "That's okay, you don't have to kiss me."

She choked on a laugh, trying to ignore the tsunami of goose bumps his words had triggered on her skin. "Yeah, you wish, Ryan."

He laughed and began walking away with his bike, turning only to add, "I'll be back for that box of Mason-Dang-Chocolate."

———

IT WAS ONLY after he and Shaan were out of sight that Sahana realized how hard her heart was beating. For a moment, she stood staring in the direction they'd gone, unable to decipher what had happened—what she was feeling. She'd never met a man like Ryan before—a man who'd figured out her trigger points. A man who could leave her feeling both weak and emboldened; someone who could make her want to laugh when she should want to frown; someone who could toy with her ego while making the exercise feel wholly complimentary.

Emerging from her waterfall of emotions, she gently reached for Misha's hand. "Come on, kiddo, let's get closer so we can watch the race."

They walked up to the velodrome, where Sahana could see the racers. Ryan looked distinctly handsome in his racing gear and the yellow-tinted glasses he now had on, as did her cousin, Shaan. They both looked rather formidable. Ryan especially, the way he walked his bike over to the starting line. He briefly looked across the arena in her direction, causing her heart to skip a beat. She swallowed hard, her one hand gently holding Misha's.

IT WAS ONE of the largest tracks in the country, a concrete oval shape of about three hundred and eighty meters in total length with slopes of varying degrees, banked corners, and only left turns.

The organizers announced the first race and the rules along with it. It sounded straightforward. The race was called Last Jack, with riders mass-starting off the starting line. A neutral lap would follow, after which riders would hear a bell from the officials, signaling for them to speed up, racing full throttle through the next lap. The last wheels across the finish line of that lap would get pulled out. They'd continue this until three riders remained, followed by one Free Pass lap, in which they'd ride out the lap without anyone getting pulled out, followed by a final lap. The rider to cross the finish line first, out of the last three remaining riders, wins.

The race officials called out some final announcements. Something about how the bikes the racers were riding needed to be single-speed, fixed gear bikes with no brakes. *No brakes?* Sahana frowned. She proceeded to explain the rules to Misha, who understood most of it. But Misha's eyes were for Shaan and Shaan alone, regardless of how he did. Sahana pulled her close and the two of them huddled side by side as the bell went off for the racers to start. Loud music blared from the speakers surrounding the velodrome, pumping up the energy among the racers and audience, alike.

Sahana instantly felt her eyes search the sea of riders for Ryan. Yup, there he was, a vision in blue, with his helmet and yellow-tinted sunglasses. He and Shaan had already ridden their way to the middle of the pack. Shaan looked right in his element, and it warmed Sahana's heart to think he was willing to give this moment up for his child.

"Daddy looks so good," Misha said with a cheerful laugh.

Sahana nodded. "He's rocking and rolling, Misha." For a moment, she didn't see Ryan anymore, but then she did. He was still riding somewhere in the middle of the pack, his taut, muscled shoulders hunched over and firmly grabbing the handlebars of his race bike. His eyes no longer tried to grab for Sahana, as it had previously done. He appeared entirely focused on the track now, his lips thinly tightening.

She watched with bated breath, as he, with Shaan following close on his wheels, moved up the ranks one by one while the last set of wheels that crossed the finish line were pulled out. Over the course of the next few minutes, only a handful of riders remained—six riders, including Ryan and Shaan. The officials announced they'd have two more pull-out laps, following which they'd have a neutral lap. Ryan was in number three. Shaan was number four. While two riders were tied in last place. When the wheels crossed the finish line, the last two riders, still tied, were pulled out, leaving Shaan in fourth place, with four riders remaining.

"Oh no, Daddy's in danger!" Misha cried, with a worried look in her eyes.

"I know you're worried, kiddo, but remember what a good job he's done. Even if he did get pulled out, we're going to be super proud of him, right?" Sahana asked, reassuring her niece.

The little girl nodded. "Yeah, and anyway, I'm beginning to miss him," she added.

But a second later, Ryan steered right past rider three and two, pinching second place. Shaan, who was in fourth place, managed to dash past rider three just in time to take third place behind Ryan as the riders crossed the finish line again, pulling the fourth rider out of the race.

"Yay!" Misha cheered, clapping wildly for her dad. Sahana tried to stay focused on her cousin, too, but her eyes kept swimming over to Ryan. She watched as he slid into first place, like a knife through butter. Shaan was now in third place. The officials announced this was the race's last lap: "First wheels across the finish line, wins," came the announcement.

"Ryan's going to win, Bua," Misha screamed, pointing at the riders. "And Daddy's coming in third, too!"

"It's exciting, isn't it?" Sahana said to Misha, picking her up so she could watch the finish. Her own heart was racing as she watched Ryan dash across the finish line. It shouldn't have mattered to her. Her heart should've remained unaffected. But here she was, curiously excited, as if she'd been rooting for Ryan all along.

⁂

WHEN RYAN AND Shaan existed the velodrome, Sahana let Misha run out to Shaan while Ryan continued to walk toward her with his bike, a smile glistening on his face—a smile she could tell was for her and her box of La Maison Du Chocolat.

"Congratulations," she said to him, when he was close enough that she could see the pearls of sweat on his face.

"Thank you." He smiled, his eyes casually dropping down to her lips, and then to the tiny gift bag.

Sahana lifted the bag up. "I take it you still want these?" she asked him, playfully.

He put on a frown while his smile remained intact. "I thought I made it clear I was coming for them?"

Sahana laughed. She extended the bag to him which he accepted graciously. "Was this your first time winning?" she asked.

He smiled and shook his head. "No. But it was my first time showing off."

A second laugh threatened to escape her, but she held it down. She could instinctively feel herself flirting with him. She could feel him flirting with her. But she didn't feel comfortable trusting her instincts. She always preferred to rely on factual evidence—what she knew versus how she felt. It was how she'd always operated, both in her professional and her personal life. She now turned her attention to Shaan and Misha as they walked up to her and Ryan.

"You were amazing," Sahana said, leaning in to give her cousin a hug first and then his gift bag of chocolates.

"Thanks for not noticing how badly I got my butt whipped out there," Shaan replied with a laugh as he accepted the bag. "And thanks again for watching Misha today while I raced."

"You know you don't have to thank me, Shaan. It was my pleasure," Sahana replied watching as he opened the chocolate box to give Misha first dibs. She noticed Ryan hadn't opened his yet. "Aren't you going to eat yours or are you saving it as an after-dinner treat?" she asked him with a tilt of her head.

He looked down into her face. "Actually, I was going to ask if you'd like to—"

"Sahana Sood?" came a voice, cutting Ryan short.

She turned toward it, and immediately froze with a sense of realization when she saw the man standing behind her. "Purab Rai?" she asked him. He nodded, extending his hand to shake hers. She'd almost forgotten about her match date with him. They'd chatted briefly over the weekend, and she'd mentioned her trip to the velodrome. Given Purab worked in Redmond, he'd offered to meet her by the tracks so they could drive together in his car to the Thai Bong Tok restaurant a few blocks away.

"It's great to meet you, Sahana," he replied.

"Likewise," she said, trying not to look scattered. Her eyes, however, drifted over to Ryan. He was watching Purab, and she happened to catch the tail-end of his frown before he tucked it away.

―――

PURAB RAI WAS a polished looking man. He was tall and lanky in his buttercream dress shirt and black slacks. His features were mild but effective, and his goatee was, well, tolerable. He wore his hair short, and spiked up slightly, from the apparent use of some hair product, Sahana thought.

Sahana administered a round of introductions around the group. "This is my cousin, Shaan, and his daughter, my niece, Misha," she added, as Purab moved closer to shake Shaan's hand.

"Nice to meet you, Purab," Shaan said shaking his hand while he and Sahana exchanged a quick smile.

"Is that for real?" Misha asked, pointing to the goatee as Purab bent down to greet her.

Purab shook his head. "It's one hundred percent real, and I even have a special comb I use for it," he said, beaming.

A comb for the goatee. Sahana's optimism was beginning

to suffer a slow death. She gestured to Ryan. "This is Ryan, my—"

"Friend," Ryan cut in.

"Nice to meet you," Purab said.

Sahana watched as the two men shook hands. And while she knew it was unfair, she couldn't resist the temptation to compare them as they stood side by side—Ryan's six-foot, broad frame to Purab's narrower physique; Ryan's deep-set hazel eyes to—well, she hadn't noticed Purab's eyes, yet; Ryan's strong jaw to Purab's goatee's chin. She still intended to give the date her best chance at least for her mother's sake. She felt compelled to, if not convinced.

"Are you and Bua going on a date?" Misha asked, looking up at Purab.

"Yes, and I'm hoping it'll go well," he said, tossing a smile at Sahana. "And your mother had the nicest things to say about you to my mother when they set this up."

She cringed inwardly but managed to smile back. She was painfully aware of Ryan standing next to her. The last thing she'd wanted was for him to know this was a match date. She had no reasonable explanation for why she felt that way. Or maybe it was because it made her appear vulnerable—or worse, flawed. Like the woman who needed her mommy to set her up with a man because she couldn't find one herself. She turned to look at him, expecting to find a smug smile across his face. But he wasn't smiling. He was looking straight at her, his eyes soft not judgmental, like she'd feared.

"Are you okay?" he asked her, as if telepathically.

His words had a peculiar effect on her. They loosened

the knot in her gut and coaxed a smile onto her lips. She nodded, watching as he smiled back at her.

"Should we get going, Sahana?" Purab asked. He'd been chatting Shaan up.

This caused both her and Ryan to turn in his direction.

"I don't know about you, but I'm starving, and the restaurant doesn't take reservations," Purab added.

"What restaurant is that?" Ryan asked him.

"Thai Bong Tok in Redmond," Purab replied.

Sahana watched as Ryan nodded. "Great choice," he said, turning briefly to glance her way.

Saying their goodbyes, Sahana and Purab headed out to the parking lot. They decided to drive up in his BMW which was parked a few spots down from her car. But just as they began walking to it, Sahana paused. "You know what, why don't you get the engine started, and I'll meet you in a second?" she said to Purab. He nodded and continued in the direction of his car, while she walked over to her Mercedes and opened the trunk and slipped off her Dior sneakers and slipped her Gucci pumps on again. When she'd closed the trunk, her eyes caught sight of Ryan in the distance, standing with Shaan and Misha. He was looking straight at her, smiling, as if to himself.

Chapter Nine

THE THAI BONG Tok restaurant was a few blocks away from the velodrome. And on any other night, minus her six-inch heels, Sahana would've been happy to walk the distance. But tonight, given she and Purab had chosen to drive up in his car, it had taken them thirty minutes to get to a restaurant which was, in fact, a twenty-minute walk away.

"I can't believe this traffic," Purab said with a sigh.

"It's a weekday, after all," Sahana said, trying to get past the slightly pungent smell of Purab's cologne. She didn't know why, but it made her think how it contrasted Ryan's warm, spicy cologne. She reluctantly pulled her attention back to Purab, again, as they sat in silence, waiting for the bottleneck ahead of them to clear. They could practically see the restaurant's flashing OPEN signage from their seats inside the car. "There it is," Sahana said, faintly. She was starving, and tired, and if it were up to her, she'd have resorted to some good old takeout that night from her favorite Indian restaurant near her Kirkland home and enjoyed dinner alone, with the comfort of her favorite TV show. But tonight, she had to endure traffic, hunger, and fatigue to determine if the man sitting next to her was her Mr. Right. A possibility that was inching closer and closer to the words *no freakin way*.

Especially now, as she watched him flip the driver side visor down for a quick peek at his reflection in the mirror—not at his goatee, but his hair, which he tipped his chin down to check with eyes rolled up. He touched it briefly, as if to check the pudding had set.

Sahana sighed, trying to come up with something to talk about while they continued to wait for the traffic to move. "So, um, where did you go to school?"

Purab shut the visor and turned to her. "Stanford University."

"Hmm." An educated man, no doubt. But he didn't ask her where she went. He just returned to steering the car, looking for a place to park. Sahana decided to be proactive. "I went to the University of Washington," she told him.

Purab smiled. "Oh great, an open spot," he cried pulling into the spot. "Thank God, I'm starving."

"Yeah, me, too," Sahana said, trying to remain supportive. *Maybe the man's not boring, or self-absorbed. Maybe he's just hungry?*

He walked around to open the door for her, which she thought was nice.

The restaurant, as they walked in, was packed even for a Monday night. "We have just one table left, so you're lucky," the seating hostess said with a smile, when they requested a table for two.

"Great," Purab said, cutting ahead of Sahana to follow the waitress as she led the way.

Sahana slumped her shoulders and followed him, too tired and too hungry, even to pass judgment.

"Is this okay?" the waitress asked, cheerfully.

"Absolutely," Purab replied. He was blocking Sahana's view ahead but the moment he moved, her eyes landed on the table they'd been assigned, and along with it, the figure sitting at the table just next door.

"Ryan!" Sahana cried out as her eyes clamped on him. She didn't know why, but the sight of him pumped fresh blood to her brain, lifting her spirits up instantly.

"Hey, there." He smiled, wiping the sides of his mouth with his napkin. He stood up as she and Purab walked over to their chairs. He wasn't wearing his race kit, anymore and had changed into jeans, a long-sleeved tee, and a casual jacket.

"What a coincidence?" Purab said, as he settled into a chair and pulled up a menu to study.

Ryan continued to stay standing until Sahana walked around to take the seat against the wall next to him but across from Purab.

"How did you get here so fast?" she asked him, as Purab's attention stayed glued to the menu.

"I walked," he replied with a shrug.

"And Shaan and Misha?" she asked.

"They headed back home soon after you left," Ryan said.

Sahana nodded, trying not to pay attention to his handsomeness. "And you being here," she added slowly. "Is it really a coincidence?"

"Why? What're you suggesting?" Ryan asked, a smile teasing the ends of his lips.

Sahana glanced over at Purab, who had yet to emerge from behind the menu. She turned back to Ryan. "That you came here wanting dinner and a show," she replied, looking right into his eyes.

This caused Ryan to let out a laugh. "You really think I'm a schmuck, don't you?"

She placed a hand on her chest, pretending to look appalled. "What? No."

But this only made him laugh again.

"Everything okay?" came Purab's voice.

Sahana nodded, turning away from Ryan. "Yes. Fine, thanks."

A waitress appeared at their table. "Are you guys ready to order?" she asked them.

Purab dove right in. "Yes, I'll have the sweet and sour tofu curry with rice. And could I get some water with no ice, please?" He folded his menu neatly and turned to Sahana.

Thanks to Ryan, she hadn't even had a chance to look at the menu, yet. Glancing over, she noticed the dish before him, on his table. A bowl of noodles with vegetables and tofu. A simple solution then came to her mind. "I'll have the same as him," she said, pointing at Ryan.

For a moment, this caught everyone—everyone except Ryan, off guard.

Purab laughed with apparent disbelief. "Seriously?"

"Yeah," Sahana nodded, watching as Ryan smiled and coolly wiped the ends of his mouth with his napkin again.

The waitress looked from Ryan back to Sahana. She scribbled something in her notepad before looking up again. "And to drink?"

Sahana turned to Ryan, as if for clarification.

His eyes were glinting with amusement. He turned to the waitress. "The Wang Pale Ale."

The waitress nodded and walked away.

Sahana settled her attention back on Purab who appeared to be stealing glances at Ryan. "No beer for you?" she asked, trying to distract him.

Purab shook his head. "I don't drink."

"Oh." Sahana paused. "I don't drink a whole lot, but I like an occasional beer," she said, breathing a familiar scent before realizing it was Ryan's lingering cologne just a hand-stretch away from her.

"Your mom said you were a lawyer?" Purab asked her. It was the first question he'd asked her since they'd met.

"A corporate attorney, yes."

"That's good. Great industry to be in, right now with so many acquisitions happening in tech?"

Sahana nodded. "Exactly. What about you?" she asked him, reaching her hand out to grab some water.

"I have an MBA from Stanford...I think I mentioned that already. I work for my family business...Night Owl Security? But I think your mom told you that already."

"Right," Sahana said with a nod as she watched him check over his shoulder. He kept doing that, and she wasn't sure why. Either he was checking to see if the waitress was anywhere near bringing their hot plates over, or he was likely looking for the exit. She knew she had, at least once. Because this was, by far, the most boredom she'd encountered on any date she'd ever been on, in her entire life. And just when she thought things couldn't get worse, her phone tinkled, heralding an incoming message. "Excuse me," Sahana said to Purab, turning to pull her phone out of her purse. It was a text from her mother: *"How is it going with Purab?"*

If she were to text back the whole truth, her mom was likely to call her to ask why the date was going south and offer an earful of unsolicited advice.

Sahana therefore texted back the irrelevant truth: *"We're at the restaurant. Waiting for our food to arrive."*

"Very good. It's going well, then?"

Sahana sighed, questioning her mother's math skills. How could two plus two be a hundred and two? *"It's going okay."*

"Just OK? Why? Are you being yourself?" her mother texted back.

"Yes."

The response from her mother was instant. *"That's the problem. Don't do that! You should never show your true colors to your partner before getting married, only after. Everybody knows that."*

Sahana stared back at her phone, wondering how to counter her mother's apparent checkmate. But before she could respond, the waitress brought over their plates of food and their drinks.

She placed the sweet and sour something before Purab and a noodle dish before Sahana. She had, after all, ordered the same thing Ryan was eating. She turned to look at him, sideways, only to have their gazes collide.

"Enjoy," Ryan said with a smile.

"Thanks, I will," Sahana said, placing her napkin on her lap. "Do you like yours, Purab?" she asked him.

He nodded. "Yeah, it's good. A little sweet, a little sour." Which was basically what the dish was called, anyway.

Maybe her mother was right. Maybe she needed to be *less* of herself? At this point, she was willing to try anything to give this date some mouth-to-mouth. "Purab, I don't think I know a whole lot about your company…your family business?" She'd hopped on the internet the night before and researched "Night Owl Security" of course. But he didn't need to know that. She was going to pretend to be the opposite of herself—a clueless idiot.

The question immediately caused him to perk up. He even placed his fork down and picked his napkin up to wipe down his goatee—not his mouth, but his goatee, specifically.

"I'm so glad you asked," he said with a smile. "We're a home security company, and we've got about a hundred odd employees, currently. Most of our revenue comes from new subscriptions, but a fair share of it also comes from renewals and upgrades."

"Fascinating," Sahana said, trying to appear, well, fascinated.

"It's a great product, what we offer, and if you're open, I'd love to tell you about it?"

"I'd love to hear about your product," Sahana said, reaching for her beer and still starkly aware of Ryan's presence next to her.

"Great, let me start by asking you," he began. "How big is your home?"

Sahana considered the question. "I live in a condo in Kirkland, right on the water."

"No, how *big* is it?" Purab insisted.

"About seventeen hundred square feet?" Sahana replied.

"Okay," Purab nodded. "And how safe do you feel in it?"

"Um, pretty safe. It's a small place, but it's in a nice neighborhood."

"Does your home have a security system?" Purab asked her.

"No. But the building has a security door."

Purab nodded his head as if he were prepping to say his next words. "If you lived in a gated community, in a large mansion, would you secure your home with a system, or rely on just the security gates outside?"

"Well, if it's a *mansion*, I'd want a security system—"

"Ah-ha!" Purab pointed a finger right at Sahana, as if he'd cracked some kind of code. "See, most people believe that home security depends entirely on the size of their home. If you live in a condo or apartment, you don't need security...the space feels small, you feel you're in control and a sense of control tends to lead to a sense of security."

"I suppose so..."

"But you're wrong," Purab said, beaming. "Space has nothing to do with security. The size of a home doesn't make a home any less valuable. At NOS, we strive to find the perfect security system for your home, regardless of how big or how small your home is, because every home deserves to be protected, because we believe the people living in it are valuable. It's what we, at NOS call"—Purab turned to air quotes—"Unrealized Human Value. UHV."

Sahana blinked, incredulously. This was beginning to sound an awful lot like a—

"That's the best sales pitch I've ever heard," came Ryan's voice from beside her. She turned to him, looking vexed, while he laughed freely, with no intention of hiding his amusement.

"Ryan?" she snapped. But before she could contradict

him, Purab cut in.

"Thank you," he said, turning to Ryan with pride-filled eyes. "You don't think it felt choppy?" he asked.

Ryan feigned shock. "Choppy? No, man. You nailed it." Standing up, he slapped hands with Purab followed by a one-arm bro-hug.

"Ryan!" Sahana scolded him. "What're you doing?"

"What?" He shrugged. "The guy did a good job. I'm congratulating him."

"No, you're not. You're stirring the pot." Sahana frowned.

"Now, I wish I'd brought my brochures along," Purab continued to say.

Ryan's eyes widened. "You have brochures?"

At this point, Sahana felt a laugh coming on. Technically, she should've been livid at how terrible the date with Purab was going, and how much Ryan was not helping the fact. But there she was, holding down a laugh while trying to stay mad at Ryan.

"I may have some in the car, should I go check?" Purab asked, beginning to rise.

"No, Ryan's just—you don't need the brochures, Purab, trust me," Sahana assured him, sitting him back down.

"But why? I think your ex wants to see them," Purab replied, gesturing to Ryan.

"No, he's just trying to be—" Sahana paused. "Wait, Ryan's not my ex," she squealed.

"Look, it's okay. I can sense this thing you two have going on," Purab said, volleying his pointer finger between Sahana and Ryan. "I mean, I'm sure you would've dated around, I'm not expecting you're the Goddess Sita or something. But if the man wants to see some brochures—"

"Yes, I've dated around, but I never dated Ryan," Sahana cut in to insist. "Ryan, tell him," she added, turning to him.

Ryan stared back at Sahana, his eyes appearing to soften. He turned to Purab. "She's right," he said, but his smile returned with a vengeance. "Although I did ask her if I could buy her dinner, once."

"Ryan!" Sahana cried out, unable to hold back the smile that accompanied it. "That wasn't an ask-out, that was supposed to be you apologizing for your bad behavior," she tried to remind him.

Ryan tilted his head thoughtfully. "That's being a bit technical, though."

"No, it's called honesty. You can't say you dated someone without actually dating them," Sahana said, shaking her head. "Don't you agree, Pura—" Sahana stopped short. The chair before her now sat empty, with no hint of Purab Rai. "Poo-rub?" she said, meekly and bent down to check under the table.

"Yes, he's probably under there, hiding," came Ryan's voice, which caused her to sit up again.

"No, not hiding." Sahana shook her head defensively. "I was checking if maybe he was picking something up. Like his wallet..." *Or a goatee comb.*

"Are you done with yours?" the waitress asked, as she approached Sahana's table.

"Er." She looked down at her plate, confused and looked up again at the waitress. "Do you know where the guy I was sitting with went?"

"He left," the waitress confirmed with a nod.

Sahana stared back. "Left? Like, out the door?"

"Uh-huh," the woman said. "Would you like me to box that up for you?" she asked, pointing to Sahana's plate.

She hesitated at first, then nodded. "Yes please." The waitress left them their checks and cleared away the empty plates. Sahana let out a dry chuckle. "Well, I hope you got the dinner and show you'd hoped for," she said to Ryan.

He didn't look amused anymore. "I didn't hope for that," he said, pointing to the vacant chair. "He's a prick for taking off on you like that."

Sahana shook her head and covered her tired eyes with her warm palms. "God, what a nightmare," she said with a groan as she pulled her wallet out to pay for dinner.

For a moment, Ryan stayed silent. "Did you guys drive here?" he asked slowly, just as the waitress brought a box over with Sahana's uneaten dinner.

She nodded, sulkily. "In Purab's car."

Ryan pulled his wallet out, paid for their dinners, and turned to Sahana. "I can walk you back. My truck's still at Moorhill Park where you're parked."

"No, thank you." Sahana shook her head. "You've already paid for my dinner and the last thing I need is to give you the satisfaction of pity-walking me back to my car after a botched date."

Ryan stood up from his seat. "Okay, how about this? I'll walk you back and you can clobber me on the way for messing up your date with Purab?"

Sahana looked up to meet his playful eyes while fighting back a smile. She considered him—his black sweater, and dark blue jeans, his height, his physique, his strong jaw. Of course, knew none of this was Ryan's fault. It likely wasn't Purab's, either. Her mother would prefer to say she didn't try hard enough. And maybe she could've done better. But regardless of the reason, the moment needed a soothing balm. And Ryan appeared to have exactly the kind of balm the moment needed. "Deal," she said and stood up.

Chapter Ten

IT WAS A twenty-minute walk back to Moorhill Park. Sahana's feet were killing her as she walked beside Ryan. Even with her six-inch heels, her head was just on par with his shoulders. As they exited the restaurant and walked down the sidewalk, she could feel him stealing glances at her. It was odd how her skin tingled each time she caught him looking her way.

"Are you okay walking in those?" Ryan asked, pointing to her shoes as they walked down the sidewalk. He seemed to have a talent for knowing exactly what was on her mind.

She shook her head. "I should've kept those sneakers on." It surprised her, how the words rolled off her tongue without effort—without needing a filter of caution. To anyone else, she could never picture herself admitting the truth that she'd overshot the mark; gotten all dressed up and changed her shoes for a date with a man who'd ended up bailing on her. But with Ryan, it was the exact opposite. She couldn't picture herself *not* admitting the sad fact.

"Can I ask you something?" Ryan said slowly.

"Sure."

"What's a woman like you doing on a date like this?" he asked. "With a man like that?" He pointed in the direction of the restaurant they'd left behind.

The question was more painful than her six-inch heels on a twenty-minute walk. "My mom set us up," she replied.

"Like on a dare?" he tried to clarify.

Now she had to look up at him. He was smiling. "Shut up, Ryan," she said, gently punching the tautness of his arm with her fist. It felt like a brick wall. Like something she could lean on for comfort.

"No, I'm serious," Ryan insisted. "I can't picture you with a guy like that. It's why I—" He stopped short.

Sahana squinted up at him. "Why you, what? Wait a minute, it wasn't a coincidence was it, Ryan Mehra? You being there at Thai Bong Tok? Tell me the truth."

He sighed. "I wanted to make sure you'd be okay. The guy looked…I don't know, shady."

"Shady?" Sahana raised a brow. "And yet you asked to see his brochures."

Ryan laughed. "I asked that to distract him from you."

"Well done, you succeeded," Sahana replied dryly.

"But why would you let your mom set you up with anyone?" Ryan continued. "That's just crazy."

Sahana cringed. They were now approaching a bottleneck pain-point in their conversation. "She wants me to get married and settle down. I'm thirty-two and still unmarried. And I come from a traditional Punjabi family where a thing like that can turn into a giant gossip magnet. You should know this, considering your dad was Punjabi."

"Yeah I get that, but I find it hard to believe that someone like you needs help in that department." He paused to glance at her. "Unless you're some kind of sociopath?"

"I wish I was a sociopath. Then I'd have an answer to your question," Sahana replied, as the two of them continued to walk side by side. She felt their bodies move closer, as they did. "But the truth is, I don't know why I've been so unlucky in love. At first it was because I wasn't looking for love. I got into law school, and I dated around some, but I was chasing a high-flying career…I still am. I'm hoping to make junior partner at my firm."

"Wow, that's great," Ryan said.

"Yeah, but, I suppose I took my love life for granted along the way. I was sure I'd get what I wanted when I wanted it because I was the perfect cousin in the family…I was the overachiever." She paused. "You know, my dadima, when she was still alive, used to say to me in Punjabi, *Raba ne tainu dil kohl ke dita hai.*"

Ryan smiled back. "Haven't heard that one in a while."

"You know what it means?" Sahana asked, surprised.

"The Lord gave to you, wholeheartedly?" he offered.

Sahana smiled. "I guess my grandmother was wrong about my love life. Because it hasn't exactly worked out that way." She paused to consider him. "Maybe I should've got around more in college like you did?"

Ryan coughed up a laugh. "You've really got the wrong end of the stick there, you know," he said. "I only meant that I partied a ton, and had a lot of friends in college, including Shaan. I was never a philanderer. Believe it or not, I'm a one-woman kind of man."

Sahana glanced at him. "I suppose I could ask you the same question. How come you're not married? Unless you have a girlfriend?"

He shook his head. "No. No girlfriend. I did have one, but we broke up some months ago when I decided to move back to Seattle. It was serious, but we weren't in love."

Ryan and Sahana paused for a traffic light. "You believe in love, then?" She turned to him, and their gazes met for a moment.

"I do," he replied just as the red light turned green. "But I go about my life a bit differently than you do."

"What do you mean?" she asked, as they stepped forward to cross the street. They'd almost arrived at the parking lot. But before she could take another step, she heard a loud horn, followed by the touch of a firm but gentle arm on her waist that pulled her back just as a car sped right before her, driving through a red light. When she turned, she felt Ryan's face inches away from hers, his hand still gripping her waist from behind. She felt his warm grasp slowly slide away. "Th-thanks," she said softly. He'd just saved her life.

"You're welcome," he replied. They locked eyes for a moment before crossing the street together, heading into the parking lot by the velodrome. Her Mercedes and his blue Ford truck were the only two cars left there. They stood before each other, next to Sahana's car, her face illuminated by the dusty white lights of the lot.

"Come on," he said, leading her toward his truck. "I have an idea."

Sahana followed him, a bit unsurely. "What idea? I can't stay, Ryan," she protested, as he led her over to the front of his truck. "It's a workday tomorrow and—"

"Would you mind if I lifted you up a second?" He stood facing her, with her back against the front of his truck.

Her heart skipped a beat. "L-lifted me up? Why? Where?"

"Do you mind?" he asked her again. His face was looking down into hers, his eyes into her eyes.

She shook her head. "I don't mind." Before she could realize what was happening, Ryan led her around to the bed of his truck, opened the tailgate, and hoisted her up onto it. She felt his hands as they wrapped firmly around her waist as he did, following which she felt his fingers slip away. Maybe it was the chill of the night air, or the effect of his fingers against her body, but Sahana quivered. She watched as Ryan walked over to the driver's side and opened the door to retrieve the small gift bag she'd given him after his win at the velodrome.

Bringing it around, he hoisted himself onto the truck bed, next to Sahana. "I've been dying to break into these since you gave them to me," he admitted, gesturing to the gift bag. He pulled his jacket off and handed it to her. "You look cold," he added.

Sahana smiled. "Thank you," she said, reaching over to accept it. *He's getting better and better at reading my mind,* she thought, as she cuddled up to the warmth of his jacket and watched him untie the fancy satin bow around the hand-painted box of chocolates.

He lay the tiny box between them, allowing her the first pick.

She looked down at the pieces of chocolate, white, dark, and milk before looking up again. "I can't stay Ryan. I should get going. I've got a meeting tomorrow I should prep for, and I should call my mother back...she'll want to know how the date with Purab went."

Ryan nodded. "You probably should. But what do you *want* to do?"

She breathed in as she considered this. She didn't know why, or how Ryan had done it, but for the first time in her adult life, Sahana found herself breaking away from her expectations of herself. Smiling, she slipped her heels off, one by one and placed them between her and Ryan, next to the open box of chocolates. She folded her feet under her and chose a white-raspberry truffle for herself. She could tell Ryan was watching her every move, a smile across his face. "You didn't answer my question," she said, biting into the chocolate to feel the floral vanilla flavor of it on her tongue.

Ryan's eyes stayed on her a moment longer. He reached for a piece of dark chocolate. "What question?" he asked, letting out an involuntary moan. "Oh man, that's good," he cried, causing Sahana to laugh.

"What did you mean when you said you live life differently than I do?" she asked him.

He paused as he held the half-eaten chocolate between his fingers. "I guess I meant that I act on instinct," he replied. "I don't care so much about what people think, or my public image, or what people expect of me. That doesn't mean I don't care about other people, I do. I'm aware I have responsibilities to live up to. But I tend to follow my gut along the way. I take it you don't."

Sahana considered this with a frown and shook her head. "No, I don't. And it's probably because I think instincts don't always lead a person in the right direction. I prefer to act on proof, and what I know for sure. I like things a certain way."

"You like things perfect," he said with a smile.

It was as if he could see through her, right down to her core. He'd known her a short time, and yet he seemed to understand her—the things that mattered to her, better than anyone else. "I do like things perfect." She smiled back.

"But what's perfect may not always be what's right," Ryan said, reaching for a second piece of chocolate.

"I could say the same of instincts?" Sahana countered. "Following one's heart can sometimes lead to heartbreak."

"Like your moustache incident?" Ryan asked, glancing at her sideways.

Sahana looked back, startled, but she let out a laugh. "Believe it not, I actually thought that one through," she said. "And anyway, how can you be sure yours is the right way and mine isn't?"

"I can't be sure it's the right way. I'm just saying it's *my* way," Ryan said, his eyes coming to rest on her. "And you'll never know what I mean, until you try it out for yourself...roll with your instincts for a change."

Sahana watched as his gaze now dropped down to her lips for moment before rising up again. She looked away, reaching for another piece of chocolate. "Is that why you changed your mind about the acquisition?" she asked slowly.

Ryan paused to look back at her.

She smiled. "I'm asking because I'm curious. When a deal falls through, I like to dissect it to understand what went wrong...what I could've done different."

"It wasn't you," he said, shaking his head. "It was hard when my parents died. It was a lot to deal with, emotionally.

Which was what prompted me to move to New York...it's what prompted me to talk to your team about the acquisition. But, when it came down to it, I realized I had a bigger responsibility than that. My parents started the inn, and I inherited it. In a way, I felt I owed it to them to keep it going...keep their legacy alive. I changed my mind about selling because holding on to the inn felt like the right thing to do."

"Even if it means giving up on the opportunity to capitalize on a good investment and pay off your loan?" Sahana asked.

"Yup. Money can't change my mind." He paused to consider her. "I know you feel differently and I'm not trying to offend you."

"I know," Sahana smiled. "And I still don't understand your reasoning. But I respect it."

Ryan smiled back. "Maybe if you knew the place...if you stayed at the inn, and really got a sense of what I'm trying to hold on to, you'd understand why I'm holding on?"

The thought floated inside her brain. She nodded. "Maybe I will sometime. If nothing else, it'll give me a chance to get away for a bit."

"And it'll give us a chance to hang out more," Ryan added.

His words caused her to flush. "I really need to get going," she said, softly.

He studied her for a moment. And she wondered if he would try and stop her from leaving again. If he did, would she give in? But he nodded.

Sliding off the truck bed, he reached his hand out to help

Sahana off. He watched as she slipped back into her heels then he walked her over to her car. After she'd tucked herself behind the wheel, she popped her head out of her open window. He stood just outside, smiling, with his arms crossed over his chest. "I guess I'll see you around, then?" she asked.

He nodded. "I'll make sure of it."

Chapter Eleven

"DO YOU *WANT* to die alone?" Sharmila Sood asked, the words reverberating through her jowls as she stood with her head bent down to her knees and the flats of her palms touching the ground.

Sahana, who was holding the same exact pose on the yoga mat just next to her mom, sighed. "I wouldn't say that, no."

"Then why did you insult our family this way?" her mother coughed back.

They were at their usual weekend yoga class. But today was especially tormenting for Sahana, considering how awful her match date with Purab went. Not only had the putz abandoned ship midway through the date, he'd gone back home and texted his mommy about it. She, on the other hand, keeping in line with traditional Indian matchmaking custom, had texted Sahana's mother to let her know how poorly Sahana had treated her son.

"Purab and I, didn't click, Mom," Sahana said, as Penny, their yoga instructor's voice, echoed across the room, asking them to drop their knees down to the mat to enter Child's Pose.

"Have your arms reaching out above your head, pulling

down gently to feel that warm stretch…" came her calming voice.

"But he says you kept flirting with some ex of yours? Ryan or something?" her mother asked with a frown, as she plumped her weight on her folded legs on the mat. She chose not to enter Child's Pose, and instead, continued to sit upright, watching Sahana.

The latter, ignoring her mother's admonishing stare, entered Child's Pose. "Ryan's not an ex," she said, her voice muffled between her face and her knees. "He's a friend." An image of him came to mind as she spoke, reviving the memory of his hand on her waist, twice in one night. "In fact, he saved my life," she added.

"Purab saved your life?" her mother asked, eagerly.

"No, Ryan did."

Sahana could hear her mother sigh, and when she lifted her head up from her lap, she saw her mother had succumbed to Child's Pose.

"Oh, Krishna, give me strength," the older woman beseeched her favorite god.

"Now rise slowly out of your Child's Pose," came Penny's voice. "Lay your weight back, sitting flat on your mat, back straight. Turn around slowly to lay yourself back on your mat as you enter Savasana, or Corpse Pose."

Sahana followed the instructions to a tee, while her mother preferred a more rustic approach—a few jerky movements as she plopped herself on her mat, smackdown on her bottom, before falling flat on her back as if she were voluntarily passing out.

"Mom, Ryan had nothing to do with the date going badly with Purab. If at all, it was me. I just didn't connect with Purab the way I'd hoped I would."

"Why do you say that? He's educated, nice looking, rich, what more do you want?"

"Shhh!" Sahana hushed her as her voice was now echoing across the room. "Look, I'm not saying I was my best on the date, but Purab was really self-absorbed and boring...really low energy."

"Low energy?" Her mother frowned. "He's a man, not a Great Dane."

Sahana closed her eyes, breathing in deep as she tried to enter Savasana and stay there. Maybe if she played dead, her mother would leave her alone. If it could work with a black bear, it could work with a Sood matriarch.

"I don't know what to do with you, anymore, Sahana," her mother continued to fret, and *loudly*, probably to Penny's dismay. "You're perfect in every way...you are beautiful, you are educated, you are financially secure, as your generation calls it...*and* you have a successful career. God has given you everything. Your cousins, when you were younger, always said how much they envied you, and how much they wanted to be like you. So, then, why can't you find a man for yourself?"

Incredible, thought Sahana, how her mother had managed to sum up her entire life, all while playing a chatty corpse in a yoga class. "I don't know," she replied.

"I'll tell you why," her mother cut in. "You *want* to be unhappy."

Sahana reopened her eyes and frowned at the ceiling with disbelief. *"What?"*

"Laila's mother-in-law, Mona Singh, even has a term for it," her mother continued, "self-destructive."

Conceding her Corpse Pose, Sahana sat up to look at her mother. "That's what happens when you get psychiatric advice from a dermatologist," she snapped. Her mother, however, had her eyes closed and was laying still on her back. She'd said what she wanted Sahana to hear. She'd pushed the right buttons, so she now looked perfectly satisfied with herself. Sahana continued to speak to her, though. "And I can't believe you've been talking about me to my cousin's mother-in-law. I mean, why would you do that?"

Now her mother opened her eyes. "It's a good thing I did, because at least now I know the reason you are still unmarried is not my fault or your father's. It's your choice." Her mother sat up on her mat next to Sahana. "It also means you can change your life by changing your choice."

"Being alone is not my choice," Sahana said. "I don't choose for my match dates not to work out."

"Would you two like to continue your discussion outside?" When mother and daughter turned, it was Penny, wearing the hardest frown a yoga-cleansed face could manage.

"We are almost done, Penny," Sharmila promised her. "And if you knew what I'm dealing with here, you'd want me to stay sitting." She didn't wait for Penny to counter. She turned back to Sahana. "Okay, then promise me that you will meet the next boy with not just an open mind, but an open heart. Because Sahana, I've got something to tell you." Her mother paused, as if waiting for her daughter to acknowledge this was a vital moment.

"What is it?"

With her legs crossed under her, her mother clasped her knees to pull herself closer to Sahana to afford a whisper. "Mohanji told me your Guru is in the Seventh House."

"What's that supposed to mean?" Sahana frowned.

"The Seventh House is connected to marriage in astrology. And Mohanji said your planets are aligned. So, it may really happen for you this time. You may meet the one you are destined to marry. And since Darsh Malhotra is the next boy in line to see you, he might be the one," her mother concluded.

Sahana sighed as pressure mounted within her—the pressure of letting her mother down again, the pressure of being perfect yet unmarried and hence a topic of conversation for all her relatives. She was tired of it. And it didn't help that the only thing that could provide her the respite she needed from her present woes—the chance to be promoted to junior partner at the firm—was a fifty-fifty prospect at best.

When she finally regained herself, Sahana moved back into Corpse Pose. Inside her head, she felt a storm brewing along with an instinct to run away. Her mother was silent, allowing Penny's voice to come through loud and clear to Sahana, as if telepathically: "Picture a spot in your brain that doesn't trigger any thoughts…"

Sahana listened. Something told her to.

"Think of something, even someone who provides a sense of calm in your life…it could be your home, a picture or photograph, a memory, a scenic view, a person…" Penny continued.

Sahana focused, following the voice. Her head was still a

muddle of thoughts; a murky swamp filled with trigger points that were connected to her heart. She felt the need to escape it. She needed to get away. She needed a change of scene.

"Think where you want to go. Think of a spot where you want to be that will offer you a sense of calm. An oasis of comfort in an emotional desert…"

As if rising out of a mist, Sahana saw something—an image of Ryan Mehra, standing in his black sweater and jeans, on the front porch of the inn, surrounded by the colors of August. Penny's voice on the outside was now replaced by Ryan's voice inside her head. "You'll never know it until you try…roll with your instinct." Sahana abruptly opened her eyes. Her blood was pumping as an idea came to her—a thought that almost felt like a solution to some, if not all of her life's problems.

When yoga class was done, she hugged her mom goodbye, promising her she'd think long and hard about everything she'd told her. She drove back to her condo in Kirkland, jumped on her laptop, and navigated straight over to The Wildling Inn website, and their "Reservations" page. She picked up the phone and dialed Ryan's cell. He'd texted her the other night to check if she'd got home safe after their chat in the parking lot. They'd continued to exchange messages throughout the week.

"Didn't think I'd hear from you this early on a weekend," he answered on the first ring.

"Should I hang up?"

"Don't you dare," he replied.

She could hear him typing. "Oh, are you working? Sorry,

I didn't realize."

"No, that's okay. I'm managing the front desk at the inn. But it's quiet right now. I can talk."

"Wait a minute, are you saying that if I were to call The Wilding Inn right now, *you* would answer the phone?"

"Yes, I would," Ryan replied, obligingly.

Sahana disconnected their call and dialed the number listed on the inn's website. The call was answered on the first ring. "The Wildling Inn, this is Ryan."

"Amazing."

He let out a laugh and she joined in.

"So, listen, Ryan at The Wildling Inn," Sahana said, settling into the couch with her laptop. "I called because I wanted to get your advice."

"Wow, I'm flattered," he replied. "What advice can I give Miss Perfect?"

Sahana smiled. "What's the best room to stay in at your inn?"

Ryan paused. "Depends. Whose it for?"

"A Miss Perfect."

Ryan let out a soft laugh. "For her, I'd choose The Queen."

Sahana scrolled down the webpage and opened the link to view The Queen room. "Looks beautiful."

"We do get pretty booked, though. When are you looking to stay?" he asked her.

"Labor Day weekend. I'll check in Friday and check out Monday." She heard typing sounds at the other end.

"Done deal," Ryan said. "Now can I ask you something?"

"Yes?"

"Is it because of what I said the other night? Is that why you want to stay at the inn?"

An image of her mother sitting on the yoga mat and fretting, crossed Sahana's mind, followed by the thought of Darsh Malhotra and the thought of restarting what appeared to be a never-ending cycle of match dates and disappointed hopes. "It's partly because of what you said that night," she replied. "But mostly it's because I want to get away for a bit. I want some peace before I go to war with my love life again."

THE NEXT MONDAY, at work, James and Candace wandered over to Sahana's office, carrying steaming lattes.

"What's this I'm hearing from James? You're going on vacation?" Candace asked, elbowing her way in through the glass door with James following close on her heels. He placed a small paper bag on Sahana's desk before finding himself a seat in one of the two chairs across from her, while Candace handed Sahana one of the two cups of coffee she was carrying and took the other chair.

"Labor Day weekend," Sahana confirmed. "But it's a break, not a vacation. I need some downtime to clear my head. My mother's cueing up my next match date with a guy named Darsh Malhotra, and I want to give this one a fair shot. I need to, if I ever want to get married."

"But this is America, not a third-world country where you get pressured into marriage." Candace frowned.

Sahana let out a sigh and peeked into the paper bag. "That may be true. But for the record, the Sood-community *is* a third-world country when it comes to marriage," she said, retrieving one of the five jelly donuts. "Life saver—thank you," she added.

"And you're staying at The Wildling Inn?" Candace asked, curiously.

Sahana shrugged. "Well, Ryan and I, we hung out a bit last week."

"Hung out?" Candace asked.

"I mean we chatted. The night of my disaster date with Purab."

"Oh, James told me about that," Candace said.

Sahana shrugged. "Ryan witnessed it and he was really sweet. He walked me back to my car, we ate chocolates, and talked." The memory of them sitting on his truck came to her mind—the touch of his fingers on her waist, the warm smell of his jacket, the way he looked at her, and the funny texts they'd exchanged these past few days. She gingerly peeled away from her thoughts, only to catch James and Candace exchanging looks. "What?" she asked them.

James shrugged. "I wish you'd admit it. You're falling for him."

"What?" Sahana cried. "Why? Because we talked?"

"You ate *chocolates* and talked," Candace pointed out.

"And you're staying at his inn?" James added.

Sahana rolled her eyes. "I'm staying at The Wildling Inn because I want to get to know the place better. Ryan told me if I really wanted to understand why he changed his mind about selling the inn, I should get to know the inn. I think he has a point. And I think if I can understand his reasoning, I could try and change his mind." Sahana paused. "I know it's a long shot, but if I can make it happen it'll be a win for our team…and for me. It'll stack me up better against Walter Cruz," she added, unsure of why she suddenly felt a pang of guilt. Yes, she and Ryan had become friends—good friends. But at the end of the day, she reminded herself, she was still the corporate attorney, and he was the owner of a target asset.

"When will the board make its decision on who gets the junior partnership?" Candace asked.

"I know they're meeting on it. So, maybe in the next couple of weeks?" Sahana said, sounding more rueful than hopeful.

"I heard Walter's playing golf all day tomorrow with one of the senior partners," James said slowly.

Sahana sighed. "It's the first thing I learned from Marissa, when I stepped in the office. It sucks, but I can't control what Walter does, or the board. I can only control my side of the story. And I'm going to do whatever I can to try and give mine a happy ending."

Chapter Twelve

THE WILDLING INN parking lot was almost completely full as Sahana drove up Friday evening right after work in time to check in. She told her parents she'd be gone for the long weekend, which displeased her mother who'd expected her to be present at their family dinner.

"And our yoga class?" she'd added with a frown.

"I promise I'll make it to the next one," she'd told her. "Our yoga class and our family dinner."

Parking her car in one of the few remaining spots, she stepped out. But before she could walk around to the trunk, the front door of the inn swung open and Ryan stepped out. The sight of him, in his flannel shirt and jeans and that familiar stubble, lit her face up with a smile. She'd texted him just before she left work to let him know she was on her way. "Don't tell me you were looking out the window, waiting for me?" she asked, as he approached her, hands coolly tucked in his pockets.

"I *was* waiting by the window, but for the mailman. I happened to catch sight of you," he said with a smile.

"Mailman, huh?" she said, clicking her trunk open.

He laughed and walked over to grab her suitcase out of it.

"Oh, I can do it," Sahana tried to say but he shook his head.

"Nah, I got this." He glanced at her sideways as she stood next to him in her flowing maxi and ankle-length boots. She felt his eyes glaze over her shoulder-length beachy curls, her mascara-laced eyes, and glossed, mauve-colored, lips. "You look good," Ryan added, causing her to blush.

"Thank you," she replied, hoping he was unaware of the effect he was having on her.

The inn looked as stunning as she remembered it from her last visit. Ryan pushed open the front door to let her in. A few people were in line before the front desk, so Sahana and Ryan took their place at the back of the line. But it wasn't Holly behind the desk, checking people in, it was an older man. "Hello, there!" he said, with a great big smile when it was their turn. "I take it you're our special guest Ryan's been telling us about?" he added, as he briefly looked at Ryan and back at Sahana.

"Sahana this is my uncle, Clive Harring, who runs the inn with his wife, my aunt, Sigi," Ryan said.

Sahana extended her hand to the man. "A pleasure to meet you, Mr. Harring."

"Clive, please, I insist," he said returning her handshake. He was a tall, pleasant-looking man with kind blue eyes and a smile that radiated up to them. Clive turned back to his computer. "Sigi's in the kitchen, but Ryan can take you around to introduce you to her once you're checked in and settled," he said, looking at the screen.

"That's sounds great," Sahana said with a smile.

"She's in The Queen," Ryan told him, tilting his head at

Sahana.

This caused her heart to skip a beat. So, she decided to return the favor. She pointed to the stack of letters she'd noticed on the table. "Is that the mail?" she asked Ryan. "I thought you were still looking out for it?"

He laughed but didn't respond. For a moment, their gazes remained locked, and when Sahana turned back to Clive, he was staring at them both with a curious frown. "You're all checked in," he said. He turned to Ryan. "I take it from the look on your face, you intend to show the lady to her room?"

This appeared to catch Ryan off guard. He looked embarrassed, but he was quick to hide it. "Yes. Like I do with all our guests," he said.

"Right," Clive said, tentatively. He handed Ryan the room key and pulled out a couple of activity brochures which he handed to Sahana. "This should give you all the information you'll need on what we offer on the property, plus our dining options, and attractions in the Gig Harbor area," he said, pointing to the brochures. "And if you're interested, we do an activity at our inn called Pick-and-Bake where our guests pick apples from our orchard here, and my wife, Sigi, does a baking class with them where she teaches them how to make her famous apple-crumble pie," Clive added, pointing to one of the brochures.

"That's so neat," Sahana said with a smile.

"We didn't always have it. Ryan came up with the idea when he took over the place, and now it's our most popular event of the season," Clive said, gesturing to his nephew.

Sahana shot Ryan a smile. "A man with many talents. You never said."

"I'm pretty sure it was a team effort," Ryan insisted.

Sahana smiled and turned to Clive. "Thank you, I'll think about it. Oh, and my room's the one with the king bed that faces the harbor, correct?" she asked, as she accepted the brochures.

Clive nodded. "Yes, ma'am. The Queen is our best room. I'm not sure how much Ryan here's already told you about the place, but yours is one of the original guest rooms we had when Ryan's parents, Mia and Adhar, first opened the place back in the eighties."

"Ryan didn't mention it," Sahana said, glancing his way.

He was looking at her, smiling. "I assumed you wouldn't care to know that part, once I'd covered the part about it being the best room in the house."

Sahana looked back with equal fervor. "I thought you'd have learned your lesson about making assumptions after the La Maison Du Chocolat incident?"

"Maybe I need another lesson?" he said, his eyes gravitating southward to her lips.

"Maybe you do."

"Right, maybe you two want to mosey over to the lounge to continue?" Clive interjected, causing both Ryan and Sahana to turn to him with a start. "Sorry, I don't mean to interrupt your er—discussion, but we've got some folks behind you waiting to check in."

Sahana gingerly turned to notice the long line they was holding up. Her eyes quietly met Ryan's. He looked as unsure of himself as she felt inwardly. He bent to pick up her suitcase and turned toward the stairway. "This way," he said, and she followed.

THE DARK WOOD stairway ascended to the second floor of the inn. Sahana couldn't resist admiring the stunning dark-green hummingbird wallpaper as they went up the stairs. There were an array of beautiful photographs, colored, as well as black and white of The Wildling Inn, right from the days of its conception. There was one in particular that caught Sahana's eye—a faded, yet stunning colored photograph of a man and woman standing outside a dilapidated-looking house that resembled the inn. Their arms were locked around each other's waist. The woman wore shorts and a T-shirt with the name Adhar on it. She wore her golden-brown hair in a feathered hairstyle, and she had the same hazel eyes as Ryan. The man was just as good-looking, tall and broad-shouldered. He wore shorts, and a T-shirt with the name Mia on it. "Are those your parents?" she asked.

Ryan who was a few steps ahead of Sahana paused and backtracked to look at the photo. "That's them," he said.

They look perfect together, Sahana thought to herself as her eyes chanced on another photograph. She almost let out a laugh at the sight of it but muffled it with a fist. "Um—and who's this?" she asked Ryan.

He pursed his lips at the picture. "You mean that handsome boy with the denim overalls and spade?"

Sahana nodded. "Uh-huh. The one missing his two front teeth."

Ryan cough up a laugh. "You know I grew those back a long time ago," he said, flashing his pearly whites at her in a dazzling smile.

She allowed herself to admire it. "I'm just glad I'm not the only one with compromising childhood photographs on public display."

They shared a mutual laugh as he continued to lead her up the stairs and down a hallway. They walked past several rooms along the way, and Sahana noticed they all had peculiar names: The Chained Maiden, The Hunter, The Great Bear. "What are the rooms named after?" she asked him.

"Constellations," Ryan replied. They'd reached the end of the hallway and now stood before a room just beside a large window overlooking the water—The Queen. "My parents, when they opened the inn, named the rooms after famous constellations."

"What a cool idea," Sahana replied, as she watched Ryan set her suitcase down to open the door to her room.

"I've always thought so," Ryan agreed, jiggling the key in the lock. It seemed stuck.

"Did you ever consider upgrading to a key card?"

Ryan shook his head, turning the key to release the lock. "Nope. I didn't want to change the integral parts of the inn when I inherited it from my parents. I didn't want to upgrade to key cards, and fancy fobs." He opened the door for her.

"Oh my gosh." She gasped as she stepped in. It was a truly stunning room. She'd seen photos of it on the website but it looked even more incredible as she experienced it in person. It had three large windows on one wall just across from her bed that faced the harbor, offering the most spectacular views of yachts and boats, and the inn's back gardens that bordered it. An adjacent wall also sported a window to extend more scenic views. The room itself was designed to perfection in a shabby-chic style that Sahana loved. Everything about the room appealed to her—the tasteful accent furniture, the distressed lamps, the floral-printed bedding that matched the white peonies wallpaper. "This is absolutely beautiful, Ryan," she said, as her eyes continued to dart across the room, taking in every lovely detail. When she turned to him, he was already glancing her way.

"I'm glad you like it," he said warmly, as he placed her suitcase on top of a luggage rack. "Maybe once you're settled in, I can give you a tour of the place?"

Sahana smiled. "I'd love that, thank you."

The moment required him to leave. But he appeared to want to stay. He pointed to the fireplace. "Would you like me to bring up some firewood for you to use later? The room has heating, but if you want I could…or not."

"Firewood would be lovely," Sahana cut in softly.

He smiled at her. "I'm glad you decided to come stay."

"Me too," she replied.

He nodded and began to leave. "I'll be back in twenty minutes with the firewood, and if you want then, I can show you around the place."

"And you can introduce me to your aunt, Sigi," Sahana added with a smile.

"I'd be glad to," he replied, cheerfully.

When Ryan had left with the door closed behind him, Sahana faced the full-length mirror on the wall. Her heart was pounding. *What's wrong with me?* She had no idea why, but she was nervous all of a sudden. It's not like she hadn't spent time with Ryan before. But something about the moment felt deeper, stronger. She'd never felt this way before. Not on a match date, not even when she sat for the bar. She twiddled her fingers, a potpourri of excitement and nerves zipping through her. Should she change? She couldn't decide. She looked good. Ryan had said so. But all of a sudden, *good* wasn't good enough. Walking over to her luggage, she unzipped her suitcase and began foraging for her teal-blue dress. It was her favorite one to wear on a night out with James and Candace, or her cousins. It was a flowy, chiffon midi dress with a halter neck that was just low enough to tickle an onlooker's imagination without giving the ending away.

"Perfect," she said to herself, as she carried it back to lay it on her bed. She paired it with boots and a black cardigan, expecting the night air would turn chilly. Her mind drifted to the memory of Ryan's jacket. She smiled to herself as she remembered the warmth of it—the smell of him on it. She checked her watch. She had fifteen minutes to go before he returned—not enough time for her to feel ready, and yet too long a wait to see him again.

Chapter Thirteen

RYAN SHOWED UP at Sahana's room exactly twenty minutes later, cradling a stack of firewood. His eyes scanned her from head to toe when she answered his gentle knock on the door.

"You changed your dress," he noted with a smile. "Not for me, I hope?" he added, his eyes glinting.

She hated how well he knew her. But she was determined not to give him the satisfaction of it. She shook her head. "I want to look good for Aunt Sigi when I meet her," Sahana said.

Ryan laughed and walked over to the stack the wood in the firebox. When he was done he stood up again. "Shall we?"

She nodded. "I'm ready to be wowed."

―――

RYAN LED SAHANA down the inn's stairway. He paused at the landing and pointed to the reception desk. "That's the reception, and that's my uncle, Clive," he said, playfully.

Sahana pretended to yawn. "What else you got?"

Laughing, Ryan led them through to the common living

room, which was occupied by a few guests. "This is the common room, and through there's our restaurant, and—" Ryan paused to wave at a woman who was standing at a table talking to a young couple. When she was done, she walked over to them.

"Hello, there," she said warmly. She was of medium height with shapely curves, gray eyes, and short, silver curls that grazed her shoulders.

"Sahana this is my aunt, Sigi," Ryan said. "Aunt Sigi, this is Sahana."

"Very nice to meet you, young lady." Sigi smiled, extending her hand out.

"The pleasure's all mine," Sahana replied.

At that moment, an inn staff walked up with some papers clipped to a notepad. "Inventory," he said, holding the clipboard and a pen up for Ryan to sign the papers.

Sahana watched as Ryan first studied it briefly before signing it and added, "Oh, and Sam, the Tucker family checked in a little while ago. Could we send some board games up for their kids and offer them some complimentary hot chocolate, please? They're in The Chained Maiden."

"Will do, Ryan," the staffer said, and walked away.

"Complimentary hot chocolate?" Sahana's eyes widened, coaxing a smile out of him.

"The Tuckers are one of our regulars," Ryan explained.

Sahana nodded. "Something tells me they'll remain your regulars."

"Ryan's great at managing the inn," Sigi said, squeezing her nephew's arm. "He learned it from watching his parents, but he has it in him to be that person, you know? And the staff really look up to him."

Sahana glanced at him.

"Team effort," he said, automatically.

She laughed, shook her head and turned to Sigi. "Ryan's going to give me a tour of the place."

"That's a great idea," Sigi said. "I hope you'll stop by the restaurant for some dinner, later? Ryan chooses the menus with me every day and he's ensured that everything we prepare here is locally sourced to support our farmers in Gig Harbor."

"I'd love that, thank you," Sahana said. She'd only been at the inn a few hours and already she was beginning to get a sense of how deeply Ryan was invested in the place.

When Sigi had walked away, Ryan led Sahana through the restaurant and out the door that opened out to the back gardens overlooking the harbor. "How are you enjoying your tour of the inn so far?" he asked, glancing her way.

"I'm finding it very informational," she replied. "I had no idea you were so good at running the business."

Ryan shook his head. "Don't let my aunt and uncle sweep you off your feet. They're really nice people and they say nice things about everyone."

"Or maybe you're being modest," Sahana replied. They walked out to the gardens surrounding the inn. The sun had almost set, but enough light remained in the sky that she could admire the beautifully pruned hedges, flower bushes, and the stone stairway that led down to the apple orchards. "Really, Ryan. This is a beautiful inn," she said, looking around.

"Thank you," he replied.

"How long did your parents run it?" Sahana asked, as she followed him down some stone stairs to the orchard.

"About thirty years, until my mom died. My dad died a few months after she did," he replied. "They bought the place in 1984. It wasn't in the best condition, but they had it restored. They'd never run an inn before, and they were newlyweds on top of that. So, it was a pretty big risk," he said, leading her down a pathway lined with trimmed boxwood hedges. They walked side by side, through an apple orchard, with rows of trees down either side.

"That must've been hard for you. The fact that they passed away so close apart?" she asked slowly.

"Yeah. It was," Ryan admitted. "Plus, I was young, and I had no experience with running a business, and all of a sudden I'd inherited ten acres, an inn, and my parents' home. It was overwhelming."

"But you clearly rose to the occasion," Sahana said. "I mean, look at this place."

"This took time," he replied softly. "And I made my fair share of mistakes along the way."

"As we all do, Ryan," Sahana assured him. They'd made their way through the orchard now and stood at the top of a flight of stone stairs that led down to the pebbled harbor shore.

"That, over there, is my family home I inherited from my parents." Ryan pointed in the direction of a stunning white house that adjoined the property a short distance away from the inn. It was nestled in the middle of a small meadow lined with fir trees. "Gosh, that's beautiful," Sahana said with a gasp. "Did you grow up there?"

Ryan nodded. "Yeah. Growing up, I spent most of my time just exploring the land and the harbor with my friends in the neighborhood. We used to stop by Aunt Sigi and Uncle Clive's house a few blocks away and she'd always have fresh-baked muffins for us."

"Sounds like such a lovely childhood." Sahana smiled.

"It was and that may be why I'm so rooted to this place. I couldn't live forever in New York," he admitted.

"I can relate to that," she said. "I'm American at heart but I have a Punjabi spirit. Those roots can be hard to shake...and maybe it's best to hang on to them sometimes."

"I agree." Ryan smiled at her. "Before you leave, I'd like to show you around the house, if possible?"

"I'd love that very much."

Ryan now gestured to the stairway. "I thought I'd show you some of the harbor views today," he said and looked down at her boots. "Unless you feel you're not outfitted for it?"

Tilting her head with sarcasm, Sahana slowly unzipped her boots and slid them off one at a time. Bending down, she grabbed them both and began leading the way down the stairs. "How did your parents meet? It sounds like it would've been a heck of a love story," she said, looking over her shoulder at Ryan who was following behind her.

"It was," he said. "You already know my dad, Adhar, was Indian, and my mom, Mia, was white. They met at UCLA. They were both economics majors and originally from Washington. They met at a microeconomics class. My mom was saving a seat for a friend who didn't show up. My dad saw the open seat, and the class was almost full, so he asked her if he could have it, and she said no, so he stood to one corner, all through class without a seat, watching her." He spoke as they descended the twenty odd stairs to the pebbled shore, speckled with dark driftwood and with fir trees outlining the edges of the harbor shore, all around.

Sahana laughed. "And then what happened?" she asked, turning back to take a first step out on the pebbled shore. The smooth rocks felt cool against her stiletto-battered feet.

"He asked her out after class. She said no. So he asked her friend to ask her out for him, which only irritated my mom, and she wrote him a real curt letter that concluded with a big, fat *no*. So, he waited outside her apartment just off campus, for eight hours and through a thunderstorm, as I understand it, until she finally caved, and begged him to go home."

Sahana had been absorbed in a semi-balancing act as her two feet clamped the pebbles, but she turned. "He stood in a thunderstorm for eight hours?" she repeated. "What kind of shoes was he wearing?"

Ryan moved closer to stretch his hand out for her to hold. "The man was on a mission, and nothing was going to get in his way," he said. "I think the scientific term for it is er—*pigheaded*?"

Smiling, she slid her hand into his, instantly feeling his balmy grip around her palm. "You mean you'd never do that for any woman?"

He glanced her way. "Not for *any* woman, no. But I'd do it for the woman I love."

She tried to look away from him, but it was hard to do with her heart beating so fast. "So, what happened?" she asked, trying to sound unaffected.

"My dad proposed to my mom on their third date. She turned him down, surprise, surprise."

Sahana let out a bubble of laughter. "She sounds like a tough cookie, your mom. She would've gotten along so great with mine."

Ryan joined her laugh. "She was a lot like you, in fact," he said.

Sahana looked up eagerly. "She liked Gucci, too?"

Ryan nodded and let out a laugh. "I'm sure if she had the option, she would've loved to wear Gucci."

"What happened after she turned him down? Did he stand outside her apartment for another eight hours?"

"You'd think, but no. This time, he went traditional and asked her to think about it, and she said she would, and they continued to date. And he waited...almost an entire year, actually, for her to decide, until she finally said yes."

"Your dad liked to wait it out and your mom liked to keep him waiting." Sahana shook her head. "Sounds like a match made in heaven to me."

"They were. At least, my memory of them makes me want to believe they were." Ryan shrugged. "Anyway, they were married...on Labor Day. And every year, my entire family—the Mehras and the Harrings, come together the night before, to celebrate their love story," he concluded.

"You're kidding?" Sahana's eyes widened. "That sounds like such a sweet tradition."

"I think so, yeah." Ryan shrugged. "Although sometimes having the entire family over at my house can be a bit er—"

"Overwhelming?" Sahana offered. "You love it, but you

dread it?"

"Looks like you've been there," he said playfully, as he continued to support her, her hand in his. They were near the edge of the water.

Sahana breathed in the fresh harbor air. "Oh, I've been there. In fact, I go through it whenever my mother hosts her dinners and festive parties," she admitted. "And don't get me wrong, I love family get-togethers. I'm Punjabi after all. I love our customs and traditions…Diwali, Rakhi, Holi, all of it. But sometimes, facing the interrogation squad of aunties and uncles wanting to know when I'm going to get married, have kids, and make my parents proud grandparents…I don't know, it's exhausting." She let her hand slip out of his grasp for an instant. She wanted to see if she could stand out on the rocky shores, bare feet, without his support. As soon as she let go of him, however, she felt herself tipping over. But before she did, Ryan gently grabbed her hand again, allowing her to regain her balance.

"You should shut them up by telling them about your upcoming junior partnership."

Sahana smiled back at him despite the knot she felt in her gut. "You know we both think alike? And that's exactly what I'd been hoping to do."

Ryan frowned. "Why just hoping?"

Sahana sighed. "Because I don't know for sure if I'll make junior partner. I might, but there's a chance I won't. I'm a candidate for the position, but there's another guy at the firm, Walter Cruz, whose vying for it. It could go either way."

Ryan's eyes narrowed. "Sounds like you have a lot on

your plate."

Sahana let out a sigh. "And the cherry on top of it is that my mom's getting ready to set me up with another guy. His name's Darsh Malhotra."

Ryan stared back. "Do you want to meet him?"

She looked back at him and shrugged. "I should settle down, Ryan. I've dated around enough trying to find my Mr. Right. I'm not getting any younger, and the longer I wait, it's only going to get harder. I should get married. So, yes. I should meet Darsh."

Ryan nodded. "I know you should. But is this what you *want*?"

Sahana stared back. He'd gone and done it again. Split hairs, and left her pining for some perspective. She was so sure of what she *should* do, she'd never stopped to think if she *wanted* to do it. She was grateful when she heard her phone tinkle with an incoming message. It gave her the excuse she needed to look away from Ryan's discerning gaze. Reaching into her purse, Sahana pulled it out to check. She smiled and looked up at him. "It's Shaan. He texted to say hi. I told him I'd be staying here," she said.

Ryan smiled. "Tell him hi back."

Sahana texted her reply and slipped her phone back in her purse.

"It's funny isn't it? Shaan knew us both, but he never said a word about you to me and I take it he said nothing about me to you," Ryan said.

"He's pretty good like that." Sahana laughed. "He would've made a stellar secret agent. Even in high school, we called him The Bank, because he was the one to go to if you had a secret you wanted to tell but didn't want it spread around."

Ryan let out a laugh. "He's a great guy your cousin."

Sahana smiled back. "And you're a good friend to him. I know he appreciates everything you've done for him…especially now with all the stuff he's going through. Thank you for that."

Ryan looked down into her eyes. "Some people are worth fighting for."

Sahana allowed herself to remain ensnared in his gaze. "We'd better get going," she said softly. "I get really cranky when I'm hungry."

A smile lit Ryan's face up, all the way to his eyes. "We definitely don't want that," he replied. For an instant, Sahana thought he moved an inch closer. But he didn't. He turned and began leading the way back toward the inn.

Chapter Fourteen

IT WAS CLOSE to six in the evening by the time Sahana and Ryan walked back to the inn. She was starving and decided to take Aunt Sigi's advice and get some dinner at the inn's restaurant. She secretly wished Ryan would ask to join her and she hid her disappointment well when he didn't.

"I would love to join you," he said, once again reading her mind without effort. "But I'm managing the front desk tonight."

They were standing just outside the restaurant door. The comforting smell of food laced the air where she stood. Looking inside, Sahana could see the place was packed to almost full capacity. "Do you skip dinner on days you work the front desk?" she asked him.

He smiled. "Aunt Sigi makes me a sandwich."

It was time for her to say good night and head to dinner. But she found herself lingering. As if there was some kind of invisible magnetic net that held her in place. Or maybe it was the clear yet undeclared chemistry between them. She knew Ryan would disapprove, but she chose to override her instinct. "I guess I'll go get some dinner, then?"

He nodded. "The Conscious Penne."

Sahana frowned, looking puzzled. "Excuse me?"

"I'd recommend The Conscious Penne entree. I think you'll like it," he replied.

Sahana considered him thoughtfully. "How do you know I'll like it?"

Ryan smiled. "Because it's perfect."

HE KNEW HER well. Because The Conscious Penne was the best thing Sahana had ever eaten in her life—penne with a delicate pesto cream sauce with notes of fennel, kale, and cherry tomatoes. She paired it with a crisp white wine that the waitress recommended.

She'd managed to get a great corner seat—one of the few remaining ones, by a window overlooking the inn's beautiful back gardens. Incidentally, from where she sat, she could see Ryan working his shift at the front desk. She tried not to, but inevitably stole glances at him. And she was equally gratified when she caught him looking at her a few times. They exchanged smiles, when their gazes did run in. She watched as he took his time to chat with guests as he checked them in. He joked and laughed with his staff, checked in on guests as they walked around the foyer, engaged with their kids as he spoke to their parents, and even carried a couple of suitcases up the stairs for an older couple. She'd only been at the inn a few hours but, already, she could see Ryan was right. She now understood what he was trying to hold on to and why. The inn was exceptionally beautiful. But she could see how good he was at running it, just as Aunt Sigi had said. He was a natural.

Of course, in coming there, she'd hoped she could change his mind about selling the inn. But knowing what she knew now about Ryan—the inn, and what it meant to him, her conscience no longer allowed her to toy with the idea.

After dinner, and a generous tip for Hana, the waitress who'd waited her table, Sahana headed toward the stairs. Ryan was still at the front desk, but he was speaking to some guests. Not wanting to distract him from his work, she decided to slip past him, unnoticed.

Back in her room, Sahana changed into her favorite powder-pink pajamas. She took a few extra minutes to go through her usual nightly routine: rinse makeup off, night serum for face, eye serum for eyes, her favorite moisturizer all around, brush, floss, rinse, done.

As she turned out the light in her bathroom, she heard a knock on the door. She paused, immediately wondering if it could be Ryan outside. When she walked over to open it, she was surprised to see Sam, one of the inn's employees. He wore a broad smile, as he held a tray before him. "Sorry to bother you, Miss. Ryan wanted me to run this up to you," he said.

"What is it?" she looked down at the tray. *Hold the phone...*

"It's some complimentary hot chocolate," Sam replied. "And fresh-baked cookies."

A smile bloomed across her face. She reached across and accepted the tray. "Thank you. It's Sam, isn't it?" she asked him.

He smiled. "Yes, ma'am."

"Have a good night."

Sahana settled into her cozy bed with her tray of hot chocolate and cookies before her. Picking up the phone she called the front desk.

"Front desk, this is Ryan," he answered.

"Does this mean I'm as good as the Tucker family?"

He laughed warmly. "I take it you got the hot chocolate, then?"

Sahana took a sip of it and moaned. "Hmm, so good."

"You know what this means, don't you?" he asked her.

"I'll need to floss again?" she asked, holding a fist to a mouthful of cookies.

Ryan laughed. "That, and you'll need to become a regular at the inn like the Tuckers."

Sahana sipped more hot chocolate and smiled. "That I'll want to do. Gladly."

―――

IT WAS THE best sleep she'd had in—she couldn't remember how long. Sahana woke up organically the next morning at eight A.M. to a feeling of blissful satisfaction. With no alarm set to wake her at her usual five o'clock hour, she'd half expected her mental clock to kick in and her wake to up at 4:55 A.M. But no. The Queen room's Egyptian cotton sheets, along with the lush goose-down comforter—or at least what felt like goose down—and Egyptian cotton, had held her, undisturbed, through the night. Even her usual nightly triggers hadn't kicked in to wake her. No night terrors from a work-related action item, no dream about dying alone surrounded by a sundry of house cats; not even the more classic reason of needing to pee in the middle of the night.

Stretching her arms above her head, Sahana wrung out the kinks in her spine, as she let out a satisfied moan. She lay in bed, watching the warm sunlight trickled into the room through the large glass windows. There was a serenity about the place that she felt but couldn't describe. Sitting up in bed, she noticed the harbor shores in the distance, and the outline of sailboats gliding through the water. How lucky was Ryan to have inherited this place, she thought. How lucky for the woman who gets to share it with him.

The ring of her phone distracted Sahana from her thoughts. Reaching across she picked it up to answer. It was her mother. "Mom, hi."

"How is your stay going?" she asked. "Are you relaxing?"

Sahana stretched her back and sighed. "Oh, it's beautiful here. And very relaxing."

"Does the place have a spa?"

"It doesn't, I don't think. But they have an amazing restaurant on the property. It's where I ate dinner last night…best penne I've ever had, and the rolls were melt-in-your-mouth good."

"Good, good, I'm glad you're enjoying it. I too have some good news for you."

"What good news?" Sahana frowned softly. Her mother and she tended to have different definitions for the term.

"I met Darsh's parents the other night. They came over to our house to meet me and Papa. Very, *very* cultured people."

Sahana nodded, digesting the words. "Very good. They sound like probiotic yogurt." She would've loved to explain to her mother how little she thought culture had to do with compatibility, but she knew she'd never win that argument. "And Darsh?"

Her mother clicked her tongue. "I'm sure he is just as cultured as his parents."

"No, I mean, how was his personality? Did it grab you? Was he interesting? Was he funny? Did he make you guys laugh?" She paused, realizing she was now reciting from an image she had of Ryan in her mind.

"Oh, I couldn't meet him. He's in California for some work thing. And even if I met him, how can I know if he's funny or interesting? That's for you to find out after you marry him," her mother volleyed back.

Sahana sighed. But before she could respond, she heard a thudding sound coming from outside the inn. She slid out of bed and walked over to the window. When she peered out, she caught sight of Ryan in the back gardens. He stood facing her sideways, wearing a checkered flannel shirt and a pair of jeans. He was chopping wood.

"Sahana? Are you still there?" came her mother's voice.

"I'm here," she replied absently, her eyes still on him.

"As I was saying the Malhotra family is very nice," her mom was saying. "And they had really nice things to say about Darsh. Apparently he visits the Krishna temple every Sunday. Isn't that something worth noting, especially from someone of your high-tech generation?"

"Uh-huh, that's awesome," Sahana replied. She watched as Ryan picked up some chopped logs and carried them over to add to a pyramid pile of firewood against one side of the inn's exterior. She continued to watch him from the window—his decisive good looks, coupled with the brawny yet demure act of him chopping firewood for his inn. She hadn't seen him since they parted ways before dinner the previous night. The sight of him now, oddly made her realize how much she'd missed seeing him. She stepped away from the window.

"It's a shame he's out of town," her mother continued. "But I got along really well with his mom, and his father also hoards stamps like your papa."

"It's called *collecting* stamps, Mom. They're not hoarders," Sahana said, tiredly, finding a seat on the edge of her bed.

"Okay, whatever it is. I am very excited about this match. And as soon as Darsh is back, we can get a date set up for you two." She paused. "Do you have his number saved on your phone? The one I sent you?"

"Yes, I do," Sahana replied.

"Good. And his mother gave him yours and she said he might even call you."

"Sounds great," Sahana said, standing up again.

"And when are you coming home?" her mother asked.

"I'm checking out, Monday afternoon."

"Perfect. I will see you that night at our family dinner."

Sahana nodded. "Yes, you will." When she'd signed off the call, she walked back to the window. Ryan was gone.

IT WAS CLOSE to nine o'clock when Sahana came downstairs. There were a few guests ambling around, going in and out of the common room. She almost immediately found herself looking for Ryan. He wasn't at the front desk. It was Holly she found standing there. She took a peek in the lounge area, and the dining room, and a quick look outside. He was nowhere. Her heart was beating faster now. But she couldn't understand her own urgency. She'd seen him just last night. But why did her heart seem to overrule this fact? Why did not seeing him for a few hours between last night and that morning, feel like much longer? Why was he beginning to feel indispensable? But before she could stop to interrogate herself further, she'd walked to the front desk again.

"Good morning," Holly said when Sahana approached.

"Hi, Holly," Sahana replied. "Is Ryan around?"

"He's out meeting suppliers, but he'll be back for the Pick-and-Bake," Holly replied, pointing to the signboard.

Sahana had almost forgotten about the event. "That's today, isn't it?" She now remembered.

Holly nodded, her brows quirking upward. "Oh no, did you mean to sign up? Because we're all booked up."

Sahana smiled and shook her head. "No, that's okay. And I'll catch up with Ryan when he gets back."

IT WAS THE most relaxed she'd felt in a long time. Following a scrumptious breakfast of blueberry French toast and gourmet coffee at the inn's restaurant, Sahana walked around the property for a bit. It was a spectacularly sunny September morning. Her favorite Ferragamo sunglasses, and oversized cashmere sweater, leggings, and UGGs set her up for success against the crisp chilly air that played with the warm sunrays. Armed with a *Vogue* magazine, Sahana made her way around to the apple orchards, and through a small fenced herb garden, where she ran into Clive.

"Hello, young lady," he said with his usual warm smile. He was tilling the soil right next to a rosemary bush.

"Hi," Sahana said, smiling as she passed him.

"Are you enjoying your stay with us so far?" he asked her. She nodded back. "Very much, thanks."

"Ryan has the nicest things to say about you," Clive said, leaning against his spade. "And I didn't realize it before, but Holly told me you're the lawyer Ryan was in touch with about the acquisition?"

"That's me," Sahana said.

Clive appeared thoughtful for a moment. "I hope you won't hold it against him, the fact that Ryan changed his mind about selling."

Sahana smiled. "Not at all. I think Ryan's lucky to have this place. And he's lucky to have people like you, Aunt Sigi, and Holly in his corner."

Clive's eyes softened. "Thank you. I much appreciate you saying so."

They chatted a bit longer, following which Sahana walked around the property some more. Everywhere she went, she was followed by a sensation of peaceful calm—the chirping birds, the rustling leaves, the smell of pine trees. When she found a hammock tied between two trees, right next to a secluded patch of rosebushes, she settled into it with her magazine. She turned her phone on silent, and opened up her magazine to read. The sun felt warm on her outstretched body, like an invisible blanket, and birds chirped around her in the trees as the hammock rocked gently in the wind. She didn't know when it happened, but at some point, Sahana's eyes closed, and she didn't fight it.

Chapter Fifteen

IT ALL HAPPENED before she realized it was even happening. When Sahana gradually opened her eyes, the first thing she felt was the warmth of the sunrays on her face, followed by a heartfelt desire to scream her head off.

"HAL-HEEEELP!" she yelped from inside her hammock, her heart jumping to her throat. Standing a few inches away from her feet, stood an enormous deer with crowned antlers wider than its girth that appeared to reach up to the heavens. "Oh God, I'm going to die!" she cried out. "Shoo-shoo," she tried to persuade the mammal.

The deer appeared confused yet undeterred by her behavior. It just stood there, staring at her while she continued to succumb to her static panic attack. But a second later, something stirred it enough that it slowly made its way back into the trees.

Sahana exhaled with relief. When she sat upright, she saw Ryan making his way toward her. Yet again, the sight of him lifted her spirits up, dwarfing all her other emotions. "Ryan?" she cried out.

"You okay? I thought I heard you scream," he asked. He looked incredible in his navy crew sweater, jeans, and clean-shaven look. He reached his hand out to help her out of the hammock. "God, you're trembling. What happened?"

"It was a near-death experience...my first one. But don't worry, I'm okay," she stated valiantly.

Ryan's frown quickly dissolved to make way for a smile. "Um, are you referring to the Roosevelt elk I saw standing next to you?"

Sahana felt her jaw drop. "Wait, you knew? You saw the elk standing by the hammock?"

Ryan shrugged. "Holly mentioned you were looking for me, so I came out looking for you and found you asleep in the hammock...and you looked so beau—er, peaceful that I didn't want to disturb. So, I thought I'd wait for you to wake up."

"And *then* you saw the George Washington elk?" she asked, insistently.

"Roosevelt elk." He smiled back. "Also called a *wapiti*."

Sahana waved him off. "I don't care which president. All I know is he was three times as big as I was."

"I'd say it looked about eight hundred pounds, at least."

"It could've killed me!" She paused to frown. "Maybe you should consider getting a fence around the property, Ryan. What if there are kids playing? That could be dangerous, not to mention it could have legal liabilities."

Ryan considered this with a nod. "Yeah, I see your point."

With her nerves until control again, she now managed a smile. "Anyway, when did you get back?"

"About a half hour ago. I had to meet our suppliers," he replied. "Why were you looking for me?"

The question stumped her, only because the exact reason

was unknown to her. But before Sahana could come up with answer, she heard Holly calling out to them. She was running toward them, waving a hand in the air, as if she were trying to hail a cab in New York. "Thank God, I found you, I've been looking for you Ryan," she said, between pants.

He frowned. "Why, what's up?"

"Aunt Sigi's just called. She's stuck in Yakima for some reason, and she can't make it back in time for the Pick-and-Bake she was supposed to host today."

Ryan checked his watch. "Is it supposed to happen at one o'clock?"

"Yes," Holly said, turning to Sahana. "So sorry, I didn't mean to hijack your conversation, here."

"No, that's fine," Sahana said.

"How many people signed up?" Ryan asked.

"About twelve? We were completely sold out," Holly said.

Ryan took a moment to consider, before nodding. "We'll let them know the change in plans. They can still pick apples, if they want. And we can offer to reschedule the bake for another day. If they don't want to, we'll offer them a full refund."

Sahana's blood was pumping by now. She'd been listening all the while, trying to gauge the situation in her head to try and come up with a solution. It surprised her, how Ryan's predicament suddenly felt like her own. She found herself diving into cold water for him, not because she should have. But because she wanted to. "You don't have to change the Pick-and-Bake plan," she said, causing both Ryan and Holly to turn to her. "I mean, not completely. I have an idea."

Ryan frowned softly. "An idea?"

Sahana nodded. "I can host the Pick-and-Bake with your guests," she said. "They can pick their apples, and I'll play Sigi's role and teach them how to turn their apples into apple-crumble pie. It won't be Sigi's famous pie, but mine isn't too bad, either."

Her words divided the expression on Ryan's face between delight and intrigue. "Wait, y-you're offering to lead a baking class?"

"Uh-huh." Sahana nodded, primly. She watched as a smile blossomed on his face. And before she knew it, she found herself smiling back.

"Oh, Sahana, that would be so great if you could actually do that," Holly said, looking hugely relieved.

"But she can't cook in the kitchen. Insurance won't cover that," Ryan said, massaging his chin.

"I'm *baking*, not cooking," Sahana pointed out. "And I don't have to enter the kitchen. Where does Aunt Sigi usually do her baking class for this event?"

"The dining room," Ryan replied.

"Great, we'll get tables set up in the dining room just as always and I'll tell you exactly what ingredients to lay out on each one."

"But how will we bake the pies?" Ryan asked.

"Everything but the actual baking of the pies can be done outside of your kitchen without the use of a gas stove or oven. It's nothing out of the ordinary. Your guests can each be assigned a table in the room which is where they'll prep as I lead them. And we can pre-mark their baking pans before they put their pie crusts in, so all you'll need to do is bake them in your oven and bring them out for your guests to enjoy." Sahana paused to think. "You know, I'd even go the extra mile and put each pie in a pretty bakery box for them, if you have it? Maybe tie a pretty ribbon on each one, and a handwritten card with the ingredients listed?"

Ryan looked back at her with mellow eyes. "Are you sure about this?"

"I'm sure." She nodded. "I want to help."

"Thank you," he replied softly.

She smiled back at him. "You're very welcome."

OVER THE COURSE of the next forty-five minutes, while the guests of The Wildling Inn who'd signed up for Pick-and-Bake walked around the inn's orchards, picking apples, Sahana, Ryan, Holly, and two of the inn's bussers, Kyle and Jigar, turned the dining room into a makeshift baking workshop. "Usually, Aunt Sigi handles all of it," Holly explained, as she and Sahana placed empty aluminum pie pans and some bowls, measuring cups, and portioned ingredients on each table.

"Who helps her with setup?" Sahana asked, as she transported some brown sugar over to a table.

"Ryan for the most part, especially with the heavy lifting. And Kyle and Jigar help with setup and cleanup afterward," Holly explained.

Ryan walked over to their table at that very moment, carrying a stack of mixing bowls. "Is this what you meant?" he asked Sahana.

She nodded. "Yes, we need a big and a small bowl on each table. Here I can help," she said, taking a few off his load.

Ryan smiled down at her. "Thanks."

"You're welcome," Sahana said. She walked beside him as he traveled to the next table. She pulled a small and a large bowl out of the stack he was carrying and placed them on it. "You're welcome."

WHEN THE PICK-AND-BAKE signees were done with picking their apples, Holly herded them indoors into the set-up workspace where Sahana waited with Ryan beside her.

"Are you sure about this?" he asked, dropping his voice down to a nervous whisper.

Sahana glanced at him sideways to offer him a comforting wink. "Come on, now. This has got to be less scary than riding track bikes without brakes?" she said, tying a flower-printed apron that Holly had given her around her waist. "Or don't you think I can do it?"

A smile now wreathed his face. "Knowing you, Sahana, I think you can do anything."

She smiled back at him, as a tingling effect rippled through her body. But before she could decipher it, Holly entered the room.

"Is this everyone?" she asked, to which Holly nodded.

"Hey, guys," Sahana began, adrenaline rushing through her. "I take it you're all here to bake some mean apple pies, today, am I right?"

The guests nodded, exchanging smiles and laughs.

"This class is usually led by Sigi Harring, but today, unfortunately, she's been held up at another engagement. So, I'm going to take her place. And don't worry, I'm pretty sure my apple pie will kick butt, just as well as Sigi's."

The others let out a soft chuckle.

"Before we begin, I want you to take a moment to grab the Sharpie on your table and write your name down on the bottom of your pie pans. This will allow our lovely Holly and our er—assistant, Ryan, here, to get the right pie back to its owner, once baked. Unless you prefer to risk eating a pie baked by one of the other attendees in the room."

Another round of laughter ensued, following which the bakers obeyed.

"Great," Sahana said, when she had everyone's attention again. "Now, I'm curious. How many of you here have actually baked a pie before? Apple or any other?"

A couple of hands went up.

"Okay, perfect," Sahana said. "The good news about apple pie is it's only hard if you think it's hard. Try and have fun with your ingredients and the bake, and it'll turn out better than you ever dreamed." Sahana proceeded to walk the bakers through each ingredient, following which she began walking them through how to make the perfect pie filling.

"The reason we're starting with this, is because our pie filling needs to rest for at least a half hour before we bake it," she explained, and showed the others how to peel and thinly slice their apples. "Mix them now with a teaspoon of the rum butter essence we've got for you on your table. If you'd rather not, just leave out that ingredient. Next goes in your brown sugar, your vanilla essence…a teaspoon of lemon juice, and a pinch of salt." Sahana paused to look up. "Some of you might be wondering why we have breadcrumbs as an ingredient. This is a trick I use when baking apple pies. I always add a quarter of a cup of the crumbs to the filling mixture here, so it can soak up all the lovely juices the apples will release. That way, it makes for a better pie. But, if you prefer not to, just leave out the breadcrumbs and you can drain the water from your pie filling before you add it to the crust. Just remember those juices have tons of flavor, so using it will leave you with a better tasting pie." When the filling was all made, Sahana moved on to the crust.

"The thing that makes the pie crust crumbly is the cold butter in it when it begins to cook in the oven. So always ensure your butter's ice cold before you begin. You can even pop it in the freezer for an hour and grate it right into your flour mixture." She demonstrated, using her stick of butter and the grater she had on her table. The others followed suit. Sahana paused to look at Ryan. He'd been standing quietly by her side all this while, wearing a warm smile while his eyes stayed focused on her. "How do I look?" she asked him, as she grated butter into a large icing bowl.

"Like a baker in a Chanel ad," he replied.

Sahana laughed and shaking her head, she turned back to her audience. "Now using your fingers, gently begin incorporating the flour and dry ingredient mixture we measured out earlier, into your grated butter. As you do this, remember that butter melts to the touch…the more you handle it, the quicker it will melt. The more it melts, the harder, less crumbly your crust will be in the end. Try to keep your fingers moving quickly through the mixture, without overworking the dough."

Over the next few minutes, Sahana and the others prepped, chilled, and rolled out their pie crust. Holly and Ryan, along with a borrowed line cook from the kitchen, Sam, helped blind bake each one, exactly the way Sahana asked them to. While they did, she showed the others how to create a beautiful traditional lattice to top their pie. When the crusts were out and cooled, the bakers filled their pies, and topped it with their lattice, followed by an egg wash.

"These pies will all be ready for you to pick up at the front desk in about an hour. Please be sure to bring ID with you so we know you're not stealing someone else's pie."

The attendees laughed, followed by a soft round of applause that ensued. When Sahana looked behind her, Ryan was right there clapping with the others. "Well, thanks everyone for coming and hope you enjoy your evening!" Sahana concluded.

"That was pretty spectacular," Ryan said to her when she turned away from her dispersing audience.

"See? I'm not just a fancy suit. I bake, too."

"You're amazing is what you are," he said, as he watched her untie her apron.

She looked up to meet his eyes only to feel him move an inch closer. But just as he opened his mouth to speak again, Holly's voice sliced through the air between them.

"Ryan, could you take a look at the oven real quick? The timer on it keeps going off," she said, popping her head out of the kitchen.

"I'll be right there," he said, turning back to Sahana.

She smiled. "You go ahead. I'm going to head to my room," she said.

He nodded, looking down into her eyes. "Thanks again for today."

"You're welcome," she replied, unsure why her heart was pounding.

Chapter Sixteen

SAHANA'S PHONE RANG just as she entered The Queen room. She pulled it out to answer, and saw it was Shaan. "Hey, you."

"Hey, Sahana," he said. "Sorry, I know you're on a break, but I needed to talk to you about something…"

"Sure, I can talk. What it is?" she asked.

Shaan paused. "I had a call with my lawyer in India, today. He told me the final paperwork came through for my divorce. It's official."

She walked over and sat on the edge of her bed. "God, Shaan, I'm so sorry." She knew this was in the works. She knew Shaan expected it to happen at some point. Nonetheless, it broke her heart to watch him go through it. "Is there anything I can do to help? Do you want me to take Misha for a few days after I get back? It'll give you some time to wrap your head around things."

"No, that's okay. She knows about it. She knows her mother isn't coming back. But it's hard for her," Shaan replied tiredly. His voice sounded throaty.

"Who else knows?" she asked him.

"You. And I'll tell Ryan tonight."

"And the family? Or at least your parents, Shaan. I know

it'll be hard, but they deserve to know," Sahana said slowly.

"I know. In fact, that's why I called," Shaan replied. "Mummyji's invited Misha and me to come to dinner Monday night. At first I wasn't planning on going, but now I think I should. And I know you'll be back for it."

"I will," Sahana confirmed.

Shaan let out a sigh. "I'll tell my parents tomorrow and I'll break the news to the rest of the family on Monday. You can hold my hand through it," he added with a dry chuckle.

"If it makes you feel any better, I'll need some hand-holding in the days to come. Mom's been working hard on trying to get me set up for another match date. It's with this guy named Darsh Malhotra and…nothing's set up yet. But it's coming my way."

"Sounds like I'm not walking to the chopping block alone?" Shaan said with a soft laugh.

"You're never alone," Sahana replied. "Don't ever forget that."

Shaan paused. "Thank you."

A knock on the door caused Sahana to turn. "Oh, there's someone at the door," she said.

"I'll say good night, then," Shaan said. "I'll see you, Monday."

"Bye, Shaan."

Sahana walked over to open the door. When she did, a smile shot up to her lips. "Ryan?"

He was standing outside, holding a pie pan, a napkin, and a fork. "This is yours I believe?" he said, extending the dish her way.

"Oh, I…" Sahana pressed her palm against her brow. "I

almost forgot about mine."

"It just came out of the oven, so I thought I'd bring it up to you." He smiled, his eyes lingering on her.

"Thanks," she said, accepting it. He started to walk away. But Sahana caught him in his tracks. "You know, this is a pretty big pie," she added.

He turned around at her words.

"I don't know what the rest of your evening looks like, but—"

"I'm off for the day," he cut in with a pleasing smile.

Sahana threw him a sideway glance. "Do you want to share a pie with me?"

His lips parted to make way for the most radiant smile. "Are you sure you don't mind sharing?"

Sahana considered the pie with pursed lips. "You're right. I'll eat it, and you can watch me."

He laughed and walked toward her. "Still sounds like a good offer," he said, passing her to enter her room.

They settled onto her bed, laying a few towels on it to catch any stray pie crumbs. They talked, in between forking pie into their mouth. "My God, this is good," Ryan said, holding a fist to his mouth. "It's not just good, it's different than any apple pie I've had. I'm not sure why."

"Cardamom." Sahana nodded looking smug.

"Cardamom?" Ryan raised a brow.

Sahana shrugged, pointing a thumb at herself. "I'm Indian-American. Hence, I made an Indian-American apple pie."

Ryan nodded approvingly. "Amazing. But where did you learn to cook like this?"

"I'm Punjabi, Ryan. Cooking, drinking, and Bollywood?

It's in our blood...yours too, I'm sure."

He smiled. "With my family, the situation's more er—comical than cultural."

"What does that mean?" Sahana asked, taking a bite of pie.

"The Mehras, my father's side of the family are Indian-American, as you know. They love their Bollywood music, dancing, loud talking, deep frying, excessive hugging." Ryan paused to create a divide in the air with his palm. "And then you have my mother's family...the Harrings. White American, book readers, joggers, quiet-talkers, hand-shakers..."

"Oh, God," Sahana said, her eyes widening with realization. "I'd love to see these two groups of people in the same room. A *small* room."

Ryan laughed. "Actually, they'll be here tomorrow. It's the day my family celebrates my parents each year."

"The Sunday before Labor Day? I remember you telling me," Sahana remembered. She let out a laugh. "Are you excited or dreading it? I can't tell."

Ryan rolled his eyes and ate some pie. "It's odd, but even with the jarring cultural differences, they get along great. Especially my auntie, Suraya, and Aunt Sigi." Ryan paused to look at her. "I was wondering if you'd like to come," he added softly.

Sahana looked up from the pie plate. She placed a hand on her chest. "Me?"

He smiled. "Yeah, you, with the pie crumbs in your hair," he said. Reaching his hand out, he pulled one out as proof.

Sahana let out a laugh and took the crumb out of his

hand. "I'd love to come, but it sounds like a private family event. Are you sure you want me there?"

"I want you there."

The way he was looking at her sent a cool wave down her spine. She needed a distraction, so she turned and pointed at the TV. "Shall I turn a show on?" she asked him.

He leaned back, knitting his hands behind his head. "Do you know we have a Bollywood channel?"

Sahana let her jaw drop. "No way!"

Ryan laughed. Getting out of bed, he picked the remote up and flicked through the channels until he landed on one in which a woman in a hot pink sequined sari was dancing in the rain, singing some poignant song about love while a man tried to hold an umbrella over her head.

"Oh. My. God," Sahana cried. She jumped out of bed and took the remote out of Ryan's hand. "This is my favorite song!"

They laughed together and Sahana automatically began moving her body to the tune of the song. Ryan offered her his hand and she gladly accepted. He twirled her around as she sang along with the heroine. Something along the lines of "If you love me today, I won't leave you tomorrow." Ryan countered with the hero's verse. "But if I love you tomorrow, will you leave me today?"

"I wonder who comes up with these lyrics?" Sahana said, as Ryan held her waist.

He laughed and gently tipped her backward. "And the choreography? They're both soaking wet. Why bother with the umbrella?"

"Oh, and how about the way the hero always throws the

heroine over his shoulder? That's got to be special effects," Sahana added.

"That's a doable thing, actually," Ryan contradicted, his hands gently traveled around the small of her back before he held her by the hands and gave her a twirl.

She laughed. "Get out. No man can actually do that."

"I can," Ryan said with a smug smile. His hands had once again found their place on her waist.

"Throw a woman over your shoulder like a bathroom towel?" Sahana confirmed, skeptically.

Ryan nodded. "I can prove it, if you'll let me."

Sahana's eyes widened. "Wait, you mean you'll throw me over your shoulder?"

"Only to prove you wrong, yeah," he replied.

Sahana squinted back at his smug expression. "You're on. But hang on…"

She ran back to the bad and started forking a few mouthfuls of pie.

"What are you doing, exactly?" Ryan asked, looking amused.

"Packing on some last-minute pounds," she replied between bites. "Done."

She ran back to Ryan and hopped around on her feet.

He frowned quizzically. "What are you doing, now?"

"Redistributing the pounds evenly."

He laughed. "Let me know when you're ready to be humbled by my sheer strength."

"Yeah, yeah." Sahana waved him off. "I'm ready."

Ryan was still laughing while her heart lodged in her throat. He bent down as if to tie his shoes, but a second later, he'd picked her up clean off the floor and threw her across his shoulder.

"*Holy*—Ryan!" she squealed.

"What do you think?" he asked, his voice calm, his laugh intact.

"*Oh my God*...I can't *believe* you did it, you maniac!" she cried out.

"Do you believe me now?" he asked her.

"I believe you, I believe you!" she yelped. She was terrified but enthralled. She felt secure in his grasp, even as she hung precariously off his back, laughing through it all.

"And you admit I'm strong?"

"Yes, you're strong, you crazy man!"

"And you admit you're wrong?"

Sahana stiffened. She said nothing.

"Miss Sood?" Ryan nudged her.

She tried to hold off answering him. But then she felt him twirl around. "*Oh God!* Fine, I'm wrong, you're strong, now put me down!"

He immediately obeyed, but held her hand as she regained herself. They laughed, as their gazes interlocked. She didn't know when it happened, but she found her arms around his neck, his face was looking down into hers. The laughter evaporated to make way for a moment of silence. Energy crackled between them, his gaze raking over hers. She didn't look away. She could've very well imagined it, but it seemed as though they moved closer, as if at any moment, his lips were coming for hers. He tucked a stray strand of her hair behind her ear. "Sahana, I—"

A knock on the door cut Ryan short. He turned to it as Sahana pulled back from him, barely on terms with what had just happened between them. She was blushing and dizzy, yet exhilarated.

"I'll get it," Ryan said softly. He walked over to the door and opened it. "Uncle Clive?" he said.

Sahana walked over to find the man standing outside wearing a puzzled look. He looked from Sahana to Ryan and back. "Sorry, I thought I heard a shout, and I came to check if everything was okay."

"Y-yes, yeah. It's all good, thank you," Sahana replied, realizing how dry her throat felt.

Clive nodded and walked away. Ryan closed the door and turned to Sahana. He appeared thoughtful for a moment. "I guess I should go?" he offered slowly. But he didn't look as though he wanted to leave.

In her heart, Sahana knew she wanted him to stay. But she was lost in confusion. She needed to think, to wrap her head around what had happened between them. She nodded. "I guess," she replied softly. "Unless you want to watch me go through a sugar-crash?"

He let out a soft chuckle. "And will you still come tomorrow? To my family party at my house?"

She nodded. "What time?"

"Six…five…four?"

Sahana frowned. "Are you just counting down, now?"

He laughed. "Four," he decided. "If you want I can come get you?"

She shook her head. "No, that's okay. I remember seeing your house while walking around the property yesterday."

"It's a five-minute walk from the inn, just down the pathway through the orchard," he said.

"I'll be there," she said with a smile.

Ryan smiled, turning to leave the room. "I'm looking forward to it."

※

SHE LAY IN the world's most comfortable bed. And yet, sleep evaded Sahana that night. She couldn't stop replaying the scene over and over in her mind—how she and Ryan had hilariously danced to that Bollywood song, how he'd effortlessly recreated a Bollywood scene by throwing her over his shoulder. Sahana smiled to herself as she remembered her own delirious screams. She'd never in her life felt so scared and so alive all in the same moment. And there was that moment between them—the one that felt like there was a kiss around the bend. What if Clive hadn't knocked on the door? Would Ryan have kissed her? Or had she unknowingly led him to it? Sahana closed her eyes and inhaled. She'd obsessed about it so much, she couldn't tell their intentions apart anymore. She opened her eyes again. Maybe she'd imagined it. Or maybe she was overthinking. Maybe they'd gotten carried away, between the crazy dancing, and the Bollywood music, and the excessive amounts of pie they'd consumed. This thought allowed Sahana a tad bit of relief. Either way, she decided, she needed to stay on her guard. The last thing she needed was to get involved in a romantic relationship with Ryan. She needed to stick to her original plan—meet Darsh Malhotra to determine if he was a good matrimonial match for her, and if he was, then begin moving in the direction of marriage and settling down. Ryan wasn't part of that plan. She needed to remember that.

Chapter Seventeen

THE NEXT MORNING, Sahana took her time, lounging in her bed. She sipped coffee and watched the harbor shores through her window. When her phone rang, she answered it.

"Hey, I didn't wake you, did I?" came Ryan's voice.

Sahana felt herself smile. "No, this is my hangover voice from eating too much pie," she replied. She realized, almost immediately, that none of her self-tutoring from the night before stood a chance against the sound of Ryan's voice at the other end. Her reservations melted away as they continued to chat and laugh together.

"I have meetings with vendors this morning, but I could sneak away for an hour around lunchtime?" He paused. "Do you want to maybe go to the downtown Gig Harbor area?"

Her heart was racing, her caution was screaming for her attention. And yet, neither one was strong enough to defend her against her instincts. "I was planning to go there anyway," she said, which was the truth.

"Great, I'll meet you near the front desk at eleven," Ryan replied.

"See you there," she replied, feeling a rush of excitement at the thought of seeing him.

RYAN WAS ALREADY waiting by the front desk when Sahana entered the inn. She'd had breakfast at nine, and walked around the property for a bit. She smiled as she made her way up to him. "How long have you been waiting?" she asked him.

"Not long," he replied gallantly.

"Half an hour," came Clive's voice from behind the front desk. Sahana smiled at him and before turning to Ryan with a raised brow.

He shrugged. "Twenty-seven minutes is not a half hour."

She waved him off with a laugh. "Should we take my car?"

He nodded as he followed her.

They drove straight to the downtown Gig Harbor area. They were both starving so Ryan took them over to a waterfront restaurant. They ate burgers sitting on an outdoor deck, overlooking the harbor. "God, this is good," Sahana mumbled as she ate a fry. "How's yours?" she asked Ryan.

"Delicious," he replied. "You can taste it if you like," he added.

Sahana reached out and cut a small piece of the burger out with her knife. "Wow, that's even better than mine," she replied between bites.

"Swap?" Ryan offered to which Sahana gladly smiled and nodded.

"I don't know if you'll like mine," she told him. But he waved her off.

"You liked the noodles I'd ordered the other night at

Thai Bong Tok, remember? I'm sure I'll like your burger today," he replied cheerfully.

She laughed as they exchanged plates. She watched him closely as he ate the burger—the one she'd ordered for herself. If he didn't like it, she'd never have known it, because he wore a look of satisfaction the entire time. She enjoyed his burger with the side of sweet potato fries. It was pretty clear by now they met in the middle when it came to taste. He knew hers, and hers appealed to him. It was only when he looked up to smile at her that she realized she'd been smiling at him all along, without realizing it.

Following lunch, Sahana wanted to see the shops, so they walked around town, stopping at some of them. Ryan played the perfect companion. He patiently waited while she stopped at every other store to look around inside. He carried all her bags as she accumulated them over the course of the hour, and he even insisted on paying for things she wanted to buy, but she refused to accept the offer. "If I agree, your credit card may explode from exhaustion," she comforted him. There was an amazing spice store where she bought a case of hand-pounded spices for her mom. She picked up a set of four marble coasters for her dad that displayed a map of Gig Harbor when you placed them all together. They stopped by a lovely bookstore where Sahana bought a book for Shaan about Gig Harbor.

"He'll love that," Ryan said when she showed him.

She bought a sterling silver necklace with a seagull pendant for Misha from a jewelry store name Free Bird. Ryan then took her to a French boutique store named Ange. "I thought you'd like this one," he said with a twinkle in his eyes. He knew her well and all she could do was acknowledge the fact with a smile.

Naturally, Ryan was right. She spent a good portion of her time looking around, and ended up buying two vintage silk scarfs—a paisley printed one for James, and a safari printed one for Candace.

"Nothing for yourself?" Ryan asked her.

Sahana shook her head. "I love giving presents to my favorite peeps. It's a good distraction from myself sometimes."

He nodded, as he held her gaze for a moment before letting go—still long enough to cause her heart to rush blood to her brain. "Come on, a couple last stores," he said, helping her with her bags.

"Are you sure you have the horsepower for it?" she asked him.

"For you, I do," he said with a wink, causing her to blush.

They walked side by side, laughing and chatting. They'd walked almost a full circle around town and now arrived at a handblown glass store named Vulcan just across the street from the spice store. Ryan received a phone call from a vendor at that moment, so Sahana offered to walk in by herself while he waited outside with her bags. It was an incredibly beautiful store with handblown glass sculptures, vases, and snow globes. As she scanned the place, her eyes fell upon one particular piece—a beautiful snow globe with a hand-carved wooden base. Encased inside the glass dome, was a miniature scene of The Wildling Inn.

"That's so beautiful," Sahana said, picking it up to inspect.

"It's a one-of-a-kind piece," the woman behind the counter explained. "We sometimes do miniatures of popular Gig Harbor destinations and attractions."

Sahana nodded as she admired it for a moment. Her gaze drifted to the store window through which she caught sight of Ryan on the phone. He was looking at her through the glass and he smiled. She smiled back and turned to lady behind the counter. "I'll take it," she said.

When she stepped out again, Ryan was just signing off his call. "Sorry about that," he said, apologetically. His eyes dropped down to the gift bag she was holding. "Here I can take that for you," he offered gallantly.

Sahana shook her head. "No, I got this one," she replied. "You've got enough bags to handle."

Ryan laughed and checked his watch. "I thought we could make one last stop at Fox Brothers Ice Cream," he said. "It's one of the oldest ice cream stores here in Gig Harbor."

Sahana nodded in the affirmative. "Yes please," she said. Nothing could complete a shopping spree like ice cream. "I'm so proud of you for suggesting it," she added.

Ryan smiled. "I'm pretty sure you'll love their most popular flavor. It's called Roosevelt Elk Choco Let."

Sahana rolled her eyes at him. "Shut up, Ryan."

He laughed, leading the way as she walked along, close to him.

Just as they were about to enter the ice cream store, however, Sahana's phone rang. She reached in to pick it up and noticed it was Darsh Malhotra calling. Her mother had texted her his number a while ago and she had it stored in her phone. She looked up at Ryan. "It's Darsh," she said to him. For a moment Ryan's eyes appeared to narrow. But he nodded. "I'll go get us the ice cream. Which one for you?" he asked her.

She smiled. "Roosevelt Elk Choco Let." She was relieved when he smiled back. He turned and entered the store, leaving Sahana to answer the call.

"Hello?"

"Sahana Sood?" came the voice. "This is Darsh Malhotra."

"Darsh, hi," she said, turning to check if Ryan was out of earshot, while wondering to herself why it should matter.

"Hey. Sorry, I know I'm calling on the fly, but I thought I'd try my luck. I know our moms have been churning some conversation about a match date between us," he said.

"Yeah, my mom's told me a lot about you and that she met your family," Sahana said.

"Mine, too. She tells me about you every time I call home." Darsh laughed. "I've been busy with work and in California but things seems to be wrapping up here sooner than I thought so I might be back in Seattle as soon as tomorrow."

"Oh nice," Sahana said. Oddly, this triggered an image of Ryan in her mind, causing her to look over her shoulder for him. He hadn't come out of the store yet.

"But once I'm back, I hope we can meet sometime. I'd love to get to know you and I wanted to call to tell you that," he said.

"Likewise, Darsh. Hope we meet soon," Sahana replied. When she'd signed off, she stared blankly at the phone as if trying to decipher the emotions spinning inside her. Darsh seemed really nice and she appreciated the fact that he'd called to tell her he was eager to meet her. Yet, she wished she felt more excitement than she did. *Maybe I'm still in break mode?*

At that moment, Ryan stepped out of the store, holding two cups of ice cream. He walked over to her with them. "Sorry, there was a long line inside," he said, handing her the one that looked like chocolate ice cream with bits of pecans, chocolate chips, and caramel swirled in.

"No worries, I just got done myself," Sahana replied. "What's yours?" she asked him, looking at his yellow ice cream with waffle bits in it.

"Sasquatch butterscotch," Ryan said beaming. "Want to taste?"

She nodded. She loved his, and they once again exchanged cups.

"How do you like the Roosevelt Elk?" she asked him, throwing him a sideway glance as they began walking toward her car.

Ryan grimaced and shook his head. "I now know to take your near-death experiences seriously."

She laughed. "Apology accepted," she said graciously, as they crossed the street to her Mercedes.

"How did it go with Darsh?" Ryan asked softly, as he loaded her bags in the trunk and opened the door for her on the driver's side.

She'd somehow known to expect this question from him, so it didn't surprise her. "He seems nice. He seems interested to meet me. But nothing's really set up yet, so…" She trailed off.

Ryan appeared thoughtful as he sat down in the passenger seat next to her. It was odd, but she could sense he wanted to talk more about it. But when she turned to look at him, he sported a placid expression. She let it slide.

They continued to chat as they drove back, and it was past noon when they arrived at the inn. Ryan walked her up to her room with her bags, lingering at the door on his way out.

"So, I'll see you tonight…about five?" he asked her.

She nodded, then paused. "Do you want me to come sooner? To help you set up for the party?"

He shook his head. "No, that's alright. I have meetings offsite till about four and my aunts are taking care of all the food, so it's just me needing to tidy up a bit when I get back," he said. "Do you want me to come get you and we can walk together?"

She shook her head. "No, that's okay. It'll be an extra trip for you."

He smiled. "I'm glad you'll get to see the house."

His eyes—his piercing gaze sent a cool wave through her body and she remembered the snow globe she'd bought at the shop. "Me, too," she replied softly.

STANDING BEFORE THE mirror in her room, that night—her last night at the inn and the night of Ryan's family celebration—Sahana surveyed her reflection. She'd chosen a geometric printed satin midi dress, paired it with boots, and a pair of ethnic Indian earrings she'd brought along.

Ryan's home was a short walk from the inn. As she approached the house, she couldn't resist admiring the breathtaking views of it as it emerged before her in the clearing, just past the orchards. It was spectacular. A beautiful white house with a front porch that sat in a tiny meadow surrounded by trees, with the view of the harbor to one side. She noticed there were a few cars parked outside, as was a blue Ford pickup truck, which she knew belonged to Ryan.

Ascending the few steps to the porch, she stood before the front door holding a bottle of pinot and a tiny gift bag. Reaching her hand out, Sahana rang the doorbell.

A moment later, the door swung open to reveal Ryan's handsome face. He was wearing a casual shirt and khakis. Sahana ignored the stubbles of excitement that had sprouted on her skin at the mere sight of him. "Hello," she said, trying to appear casual.

He smiled, the effect of it touching the corners of his eyes. "You look beautiful," he said, unreservedly. He opened the door to let her in.

"Thanks," she said, feeling herself blush.

He smiled down at the wine and gift bag. "Wow, you sure know how to come prepared."

She shrugged. "It's nothing much," she replied, handing him the wine first. She wanted to reserve the gift bag for a little later, once she'd settled in. She didn't want to do it in a rush.

"Sahana, you made it!" came Holly's voice as she walked into the foyer. "Gosh, I love the dress, and your earrings."

"Thanks," Sahana replied, aware of Ryan's eyes on her.

"Come on, I'll introduce you to everyone," he said, leading her in toward the sounds of chatter, laughter, and music that wafted from inside the house.

"Sounds like you've got quite a party going on in there," Sahana said.

Holly laughed. "Next to Christmas and Thanksgiving, I'd say this is one of our pre-holiday highlight events."

Ryan's home was almost as beautiful on the inside as it was on the outside. The interiors—the furniture, the wallpaper, the stone fireplace, the paintings, the photographs of what appeared to be his family, all melded together with the smell of dinner cooking, firewood, and cinnamon candlesticks. "This is such a lovely home, Ryan," Sahana said, as he led her into the living room.

He turned to her, as she walked by his side. "Thanks. I'm glad you think so."

She smiled up at him before turning her attention to his relatives that were gathered in the room, eating, drinking, laughing—holding an uncanny resemblance to a Sood-family shindig. Soft fusion music flowed out of mounted speakers on the walls, into the warmly lit room with the gorgeous wood-burning stone fireplace. Ryan guided her from one end of the spacious living room to the other, making introductions along the way, starting with his aunt, Diane, older sister to Mia and Sigi.

"Such a pleasure to meet a girlfriend of Ryan's," Diane said, arms outstretched to embrace Sahana.

"Oh, I'm not his girlfriend," Sahana replied, turning a deep shade of pink.

Diane pulled back as if surprised. "Are you sure?" she

asked. "Because you're just his type."

"I-I'm pretty sure," Sahana stuttered, turning to Ryan for assistance.

He wore a big smile on his face. "This is the subdued side of my family. Wait till you meet the Mehras," he said, bending down to whisper to her. She smiled to herself and shook the older woman's hand.

Diane now tapped on the shoulder of the man behind her. "This is my husband, Phil," she added. He was chatting with someone, and he turned.

"This is Sahana, Ryan's special friend," Diane told him.

"I'm not a special friend," she tried to clarify.

"Very nice to meet you, anyway," Phil said, gleefully.

Sahana gingerly shook his hand as she turned to catch a look of amusement on Ryan's face.

Next, he introduced her to Diane and Phil's three kids. "These are my cousins, Chase, Patrick, and Paige...guys, this is Sahana." They shook hands following which she was introduced to Holly's parents, Jim, who was Mia's older brother, and his wife, Trish.

Somewhere between the introductions, Ryan herded Sahana over to a quiet study. "I thought you could use some air before you meet the Mehras," he said.

Sahana let out a soft laugh. "I think your family's amazing. Just the fact that they all took the time to show up here tonight to celebrate your parents?"

Ryan nodded with a smile. "I suppose that's true."

They were standing by a window that faced the open meadows, a shaded lamp pouring a soft yellow light on their faces. They could still hear the guests in the room next door, but Sahana thought this would be a good moment to give him the gift bag. "This is for you," she said, holding it out to him.

He looked down at it and back up at her with surprise. "For me?" he asked before accepting it. "Thank you."

She watched as he carefully pulled the gold-trimmed cardboard box out of the bag. He set the box on a table next to them and opened it to pull out the snow globe she'd bought at the Gig Harbor store.

Ryan looked up at her eyes brimming with a smile. "Sahana…" He gasped. "I don't know what to say. This is—you are incredible. Thank you."

She shrugged. "You know what this means, right?"

He smiled. "That I'm one of your favorite peeps?"

A warm feeling spread across her. She nodded. "Exactly."

Ryan shook his head at her and let out a soft chuckle. "Where did you even find this?"

"At the Vulcan, downtown. They create handblown glass snow globes, and they sometimes create miniature versions of popular inns and tourist spots in Gig Harbor. I just happened to notice they had one of the inn and I bought it while you were on the phone."

Ryan smiled at her and turned the globe to activate the flakes. He looked down into her eyes. "I love it, Sahana."

She looked up at him. She could see herself in his eyes. At that very moment, her heart began to pound in a manner she didn't quite recognize. As if it wasn't beating for the purpose of beating, but as if to signal a deeper feeling inside her that somehow traced itself back to Ryan. This scared her, only because she'd never felt this way about anyone—any man. She tried to remember the coaching she'd given herself the night before. She needed to steer them back on course. "We should probably get back in there," she said, gesturing to the party room.

Ryan appeared thoughtful, but he nodded. "Can I get you something to drink? You know, before we meet the Mehra side of the family?" he asked.

"I'd love a beer if you have it," Sahana replied. "And I'll meet you back in there with the others."

"You got it."

As Sahana walked back into the room full of guests, she caught the attention of Sigi who walked up to her with a smile. "I'm so glad you could make it," she said, as she gave Sahana a warm hug.

"Thank you for having me," Sahana replied.

"Have you met Ryan's auntie on his father's side?" Sigi asked her, turning to the lady in a bright cobalt-blue sari and gold earrings. "This is Adhar's older sister, Suraya."

The woman was of medium height and wore her charcoal-black hair in soft, tamed curls that fell down to her shoulders.

Sahana's natural instincts kicked in and she wondered if she should touch Suraya's feet the traditional way. Before she could make her mind up, however, Suraya extended her hand to her. "A pleasure to meet you," she said, warmly.

"Likewise, Auntie," Sahana said.

"I didn't know Ryan had a girlfriend?" Suraya asked her. "In fact, he's never brought any girl home, so you must be extra special."

Oh dear. Sahana felt the urgent need to respond. But before she could, Sigi came to her aid, in the nick of time.

"Sahana and Ryan are good friends. She's a corporate attorney."

Suraya raised a brow. "Are you? Well, the only friend of Ryan's I know is his closest friend, since his college days, Shaan Sood," Suraya said.

"I'm Shaan's cousin," Sahana said with a smile.

"Oh, really? What a small world," Suraya cried. She pointed to an older man standing by a corner, chatting with Clive. "That's my husband, Dilbar," she said, and turned to the two young women sitting on the couch, chatting with Chase and Patrick. "Those are our daughters, Maya and Kiara."

Suraya gently knit arms with Sahana. "So? Are you married?"

Sahana smiled. The question—the moment, and the people, felt warmly familiar. It was as if she were back among her Sood clan. She felt right at home. "No, I'm not married yet, Auntie. I've got a pretty busy career in corporate law, so I haven't had the time to find the right guy to marry." This was brilliant. Same template, different audience.

"Now, give the girl a chance to settle in, will you?" Sigi waved Suraya off.

At that very moment, Ryan appeared out of the adjoining room, carrying two beers. He considered his auntie's arm-in-arm position with Sahana as he handed her the beer. He leaned in. "Do you need rescuing?" he whispered.

Sahana smiled. "No, I got this, thanks," she whispered back.

Chapter Eighteen

UNDER THE LIGHT of a glorious full moon, with strings of yellow lights hanging above them, the Mehras and the Harrings sat around the large sixteen-seater table on the back porch sharing a fantastic dinner spread—everything from a large vegetarian casserole dish, curried potatoes, warm rolls, crunchy string beans, samosas, naans, curries, and a lovely red wine that paired perfectly with their dinner.

Sitting between Ryan and Holly, with the added comfort of two outdoor heaters and the homely dinner, Sahana felt a sense of soothing comfort, enough to make her smile radiantly. Enough for Ryan to take notice. "You look like you're actually enjoying this."

"I absolutely am," she replied with a firm nod.

"Does this mean the Mehras and the Harrings haven't scared you off?" he asked.

"Considering how similar they are to the Soods? No, they haven't," she said with a laugh, reaching for her wineglass.

He watched her take a sip, setting off a tingly feeling under her skin. Lucky for her, the warmth of her wine helped soothe the effect his eyes were having on her. The tinkle of glasses forced her to break away from his gaze. She turned to face Clive as he stood up, holding his glass.

"This is one of my favorite times in the year, when we, the Harrings and the Mehras, get together to celebrate our memory of beloved Mia and Adhar. They had a special love between them, as we all know. But tonight, along with toasting them, I want to toast Ryan, who's managed to keep the legacy of his parents alive. The inn was their dream..." Clive paused, appearing to hold back tears. "I witnessed those early days when Adhar would stand outside chopping firewood for the rooms, while Mia baked pies in the kitchen."

The words rang in Sahana's ears as she connected the dots in her head. An image of Ryan chopping wood came to mind. Instinctively, she turned to look at him. But he'd beaten her to the punch. His eyes were already on her as his uncle continued to speak.

"Ryan, we want you to know, we're proud of everything you've done...for the inn, and for your parents. Here's to Mia and Adhar."

Everyone raised their glasses. "To Mia and Adhar!" they toasted together before turning to clink their glasses with each other.

Sahana clicked her glass with Holly and turned to Ryan who'd taken it all in in quiet silence. "Cheers," she said, raising her glass.

He smiled, touching his glass to hers. "Cheers."

THE NIGHT ROLLED on, as Sigi and the others began sharing

anecdotes about Adhar and Mia, including the famous incident of him braving a thunderstorm for her. When they'd eaten all they could eat, laughed, and shared their stories, and done justice to all four opened wine bottles, the party spread across the backyard and back porch.

Ryan hung close to Sahana on the porch steps, as the moon rose in a gorgeous night sky. Some of his cousins, led by Suraya, turned on some Bollywood music. Everyone—the Mehras and Harrings, alike, joined in either by dancing, clapping, and cheering the dancers on. Sahana admired how the two families blended in so effortlessly that you almost couldn't tell them apart. Ryan had been right about that. The Mehras and the Harrings were different, and yet they shared a deep, human connection that had begun with a love story. Sahana clapped her hands and laughed as Clive twirled Sigi around to a popular Bollywood song about a boy and a girl who get locked in a cabin together and end up falling in love. Ryan, who was standing next to her, cheered them on with a two-handed whistle. He turned to her. "What say we give these oldie-goldies a run for their money?" he asked, offering her his hand.

Sahana coughed up an unsure laugh. "I don't know, Ryan…"

"Don't tell me you're shy all of a sudden?" he frowned playfully.

She squinted back with a smile. "No, I'm not shy." She'd been sitting on the porch, and she stood up to offer him her hand.

Suraya hooted, as did the others, when Ryan spun Sahana around to the center, while Clive and Sigi continued their dance.

The dancing, the laughter continued into the late hours of the evening. By nine, the party began to wind down. "I should probably get going," Sahana said to Ryan.

"Why don't you stay for a bit? I'll walk you back to the inn," he offered.

She considered it, the softness in his eyes and the way they glazed over her. She smiled back. "Okay."

When the last guest had left, Ryan and Sahana settled into his couch in the living room.

He sat next to her, as she lay her head back. She admired the gorgeous wooden beams that ran across the vaulted ceiling of the room. It accented the stone fireplace, the built-in bookshelves, the large dome-shaped windows. "Should I pour us some wine? I think there's half a bottle left over?"

She nodded. "Yes, please."

Ryan got up only to return a few seconds later with an opened bottle of merlot and two wineglasses. He poured some out for her and some for himself.

Sahana sipped her wine, allowing it to glide smooth and warm down her throat. She rested her glass on the table. "I had a really nice time tonight, Ryan. Thanks for inviting me," she said, resting her head on the back of the sofa, while keeping her eyes on the ceiling above. She felt Ryan's gaze on her and it was confirmed when she turned to him.

"Me too." He smiled, pausing to sip his wine before setting his glass down on the coffee table. "Are you heading back tomorrow?"

She sighed. "Yup. Back to the grind."

"And when will you hear about that promotion?" he

asked.

Between the serenity of the inn and Ryan's company, Sahana had managed not to think about her impending meeting with George. Now, with her time at the inn nearing its end, she felt her nerves swell with anxiety as she considered Ryan's question. "I should know soon I think."

"Will you let me know when you hear about it?" Ryan asked warmly.

She watched him. By now, his gaze had slid down to her lips. "Why?" she asked softly.

"Because I'm rooting for you. I thought you'd know by now, Sahana. I've been rooting for you all along," he replied, his eyes unflinching.

Her heart was galloping inside her chest. She could feel the energy between them—quiet, yet powerful. It scared her, and yet she couldn't deny she found it beautiful. She felt that deep, unfamiliar feeling again as her heart continued to race. She worried her instincts were assuming control over her judgment. And yet, she felt powerless against the shift. Her body gravitated toward Ryan, and his, toward her. She tried feebly to talk her way of out of it. "How can you be so sure I'm worth rooting for?" she asked him, her voice coming out as an unintended whisper.

He smiled, his lips inching closer. His gaze held hers. "Because you're perfect. Not because of what you do or the way you do it. You're perfect as you are."

When Ryan's lips closed in on hers, Sahana succumbed to the feeling of falling. She wrapped her arms around his neck as he pulled her into his. She felt her body erupt with desire, as he kissed her, and she kissed him back, softly at first and harder, as the intensity between them unfolded. It was as if it had been living inside her all this while and was now, coming alive. She tried to remind herself of her earlier protocol—something about staying on her guard; something about not falling for Ryan so she could stick with her plan to find a husband and settle down. But it was like trying to glue bits of paper together while skydiving.

Ryan threaded his fingers into her loose hair, grazing her scalp as they went in. Sahana felt herself quiver to his touch as the tingling feeling she'd felt between her legs blossomed into a deeper ache. He whispered her name into her neck as he pressed his readiness against her, shushing the ache between her legs while setting her skin on fire. She let out a soft moan, as Ryan's hands traveled downward. His lips met hers again, muffling the soft cry that tried to slip out of her as he squeezed one of her swollen breasts. Ryan's hands were quick to support her quivering body as he now helped her off the couch. They kissed their way to his bedroom, bumping into furniture along the way. Crashing into his bed, Sahana kicked her shoes off, as did he. They cast aside the larger pieces of clothing between them—her dress, his sweater and jeans.

She allowed his lips to take a V.I.P tour of her body, shedding smaller inhibitors on the way. He unhooked her satin bra, taking her breast in his mouth just as it came free. She moaned and wrapped her legs tighter around him, giving him the permission he needed to do it all over again with the other breast. In the end, nothing remained between them as they lay skin to skin. Sahana winced under him, as they lay fused together in his sheets. His body moved with hers to a mutual rhythm until they touched the peak of satisfaction, whispering each other's name at their journey end.

Ryan fell back next to Sahana, leaving her body feeling electric and rejuvenated as she lay back to savor the aftereffects of their lovemaking. Reaching out, he pulled her close to kiss her forehead. She rested her head on his chest. "I was right all along," he said between pants.

She lifted her head up at him. "Right about what?"

"That you're perfect." He smiled.

She giggled into his chest. "And I should've known."

"Known what?"

"That you're a liar."

He pulled her face up in his palms to look into her eyes. "Why am I being called a liar, Miss Sood?"

"Because you said you would walk me home if I stayed on for a bit." She gestured to their naked bodies. "Is this us walking home?"

He laughed, pretending to close his eyes. "A slight delay in a man's plans doesn't make him a liar."

"What are you saying? You're going to walk me home tonight?"

He tucked her in his arms. "Eventually."

Chapter Nineteen

SAHANA NEVER MADE it back to her room. She and Ryan remained entwined in his sheets for the rest of that night, their passion cushioned by pillow talk in the in-betweens. They'd always shared a connection. But tonight, it felt to Sahana as if a new dimension had been added to that connection. One that felt deeper, stronger.

They emerged from their euphoric state only when hunger beckoned. They sat on the kitchen counter eating leftovers from the party that night, and afterward, took a midnight walk down to the harbor by Ryan's house. With the high tide in, they sat on the rocks with their fingers intertwined and bodies leaning against each other. They talked, laughed, and kissed like they were teenagers again, happy to be happy.

With her back against him, Sahana closed her eyes to a chilly breeze. She turned away from it to face him. She wrapped her arms around his waist, allowing her face to sink into his chest. His arms enclosed her. And for a moment she felt a sense of happiness like she'd never experienced before.

"I'm so glad you decided to come stay at the inn," he said.

She looked up at him. "What if I hadn't?"

He smiled. "I would've found another way to get to you."

Suddenly, a knot lodged in her throat. "Ryan, there's something you should know," she said. "I don't know what you'll think of me when I tell you this…but I want to be honest."

He frowned softly. "What is it?"

Sahana chewed on her lip, lining up her words. "I decided to stay at the inn hoping to change your mind about wanting to sell. I-I was chasing the promotion, and I felt like if I could get you to agree to an acquisition, I'd be able to impress my board and my client, and…" Sahana shook her head. "I'm sorry." She was afraid to meet his eyes. She was ashamed of her motives when she thought of them, now. This surprised her, of course. She'd been unapologetic in the way she'd chased her career goals. But Ryan had exposed a side of her she didn't even know existed—a compassionate side to the corporate attorney.

A sense of relief, however, flooded her when he laughed. She looked up into his eyes. "You think I didn't know that?" he asked, smiling.

"Y-you're not mad?" she asked him.

"Why would I be mad? You were doing your job and technically I was the one that suggested it. You did what you thought was best for you like I did what I thought was best for me. I'm just glad we ended up meeting in the middle." He sank his fingers into her hair.

She closed her eyes as she felt his lips touch hers. She kissed him back.

"There's something I need to tell you, too," he now said.

She frowned. "Oh, God, what is this turning into?"

He smiled. "Do you remember my olive branch? The one I gave you when I visited your office that day?"

Sahana squinted back. "Uh-huh."

"It was meant to be an ask-out."

Sahana covered her face with her palms to hide her flushed cheeks. "Oh my God, James was right." She looked back at him. "You planned to ask me out?"

He nodded. "The day you came to the inn, I was...I don't know, you blew my mind. I couldn't stop thinking about you after you left. I knew I had to see you again. So, I decided I'd stop by your office and ask you out."

Sahana shook her head. "Why didn't you?"

He shrugged. "When I saw you in your suit and in your swanky office, I felt a deep sense of respect for you...what you'd achieved and who you were. I felt like I'd be insulting you, not to mention, making a fool of myself by asking you out in your office like that. It almost felt unprofessional."

She smiled at him. "I appreciate that."

"But I was trying to find another way to get to you, and—"

"That's when the race happened?" she offered.

He paused to consider her for a moment. "Regardless of how it all came about, Sahana, I want you to know that I'm all in and I don't ever want to let go."

She could feel herself drowning in his gaze. His words had set off her heart again. And yet, she couldn't bring herself to say anything. She rested her head on his chest as she slowly connected the thoughts inside her brain. The realization scared her. She'd jumped in with Ryan. She'd gone off course and ended up in a relationship when she should've been cueing up to find a man to marry. Where did Darsh feature in all of this? Sure, nothing had happened with Darsh yet, but things were in the works. If she were to meet him, if it were to work out, what then? Would she turn away from marriage, so close to the finish line and end up in a relationship with Ryan with no safety net? None of this would've happened if she'd done what she should've done instead of what she wanted to do. She'd allowed her instincts to dictate the course of her actions. And now, here she was, lost.

"You okay?" Ryan asked her, as if telepathically.

She nodded quickly. "Yeah. I'm just cold. Maybe we should head back."

THE SUNLIGHT KISSED Sahana's eyes open the next morning. Stretching her arms over her head, she immediately felt the warmth of Ryan's body against hers. He was still asleep, it seemed, so she slid out of bed. Her feet touched the cool wooden floor and she walked over to the window closest to her to look outside. It was a stunning view of the harbor. And despite the muddle of thoughts inside her head, Sahana had yet again managed to find the best sleep of her life in Ryan's bed. If she was less practical, she could've easily been led to believe that he was the lotion to all of her life's dryness.

Sahana turned around away from the window to look at Ryan. He appeared fast asleep. She pulled on her tights and

Ryan's sweater off the floor, slipped her boots on and grabbed her cell phone out of her purse before heading out the door. She needed some fresh air. She'd spent the most beautiful night last night with perhaps the most incredible man she'd ever met. And yet, here she was, sick to her stomach and lost inside her head.

She walked out the front door, and down the steps of Ryan's front porch and headed out into the open stretch of meadows and trees that lined the property. It was eight in the morning and the September sun made the dew drops glisten on the leaves. The air felt bold and fresh. Sahana filled her lungs with it. She looked up at the tops of the trees, and listened as the birds chirped around her. She walked up to a line of trees and found one to lean up against. Something caught her eye on the trunk of another tree, a few feet away. She frowned and moved in to take a closer look. She smiled softly when she realized what it was—a heart carved on the trunk with the initials A and M inside it. *A* for Adhar. *M* for Mia, she mused. She felt a sting of tears as her finger traced the carved-out edges.

The sound of an incoming call on her cell phone startled her. She looked down at it. It was her mother calling. The older woman knew Sahana never slept in. Not even on holidays. She stared blankly down at the caller ID. She couldn't bring herself to swipe right, however. She decided to let it slide to voicemail, promising herself she'd call her mother back when she was back in her room later that day.

When she walked back to the house, she found Ryan standing on the porch with his hands crossed about his chest. He smiled when he saw her and walked down the steps to meet her halfway. "Hey, I was beginning to worry where you were," he said. He laid a soft kiss on her lips and frowned down at her playfully. "That looks like my sweater," he said, pointing.

She smiled weakly. "It is. Do you mind?"

"I don't mind if you're the one wearing it." He paused to consider her expression. "Are you okay?" he asked.

Boy, did he know her well. "I'm fine," she said. She knew this wasn't the truth. She knew they needed to talk. She just didn't feel ready for it yet. At that moment, her phone rang again. In the time that she'd walked back, her mother had left her a voicemail and sent her two text messages. This was her third attempt to reach Sahana.

"It's my mom," she said to Ryan.

"Aren't you going to answer it?" he said. "It could be important."

Sahana sighed, looking down at her phone. "I guess."

"I'll go make us some coffee." Ryan smiled. Leaning in, he kissed her forehead before heading back up the stairs into his house.

Sahana walked over to the porch and found a chair to sit in. She called her mother back.

"Hey, Mom," she said.

"Sahana?" Sharmila cried. "I have been trying to call you, why didn't you pick up the phone?"

"Sorry, I, er—"

"Never mind, I called to tell you Darsh is coming to meet you today," she said hurriedly.

Sahana stood up from her chair. "What do you mean? Meet me where?"

Her mother paused. "The place where you are staying...that inn. I gave him the address that you gave me for it. He's back from California and he was so sweet and so excited to meet you, he offered to drive up to your inn and meet you there for lunch. It's all set up."

"B-but I..." Sahana's head was spinning as conflicting thoughts bombarded her from within. She pressed her cool palm against her throbbing brow. She couldn't bear to tell her mother about Ryan. She couldn't imagine telling Ryan about Darsh. But then again, this was her chance to find a husband—meet a man who could prove to be a good matrimonial match. Darsh Malhotra was a lawyer, he came from a well-bred Punjabi family, he was successful, good-looking, and looking for a wife. How could she not give the meeting a chance? "I'm checking out today," she said, as if trying to find some middle ground to stand on.

"I told Darsh about that. He said he will meet you at eleven thirty. You can check out and then maybe you two can eat lunch at that restaurant you said had the best penne pasta," her mother replied.

Sahana breathed out. It appeared her mother's thoughts were nicely lined up against the barracks, ready to fire at a moment's notice. Unlike hers, which were poorly caffeinated and begging for clarity.

"Sahana?" came her mother's voice. "Are you listening?" her mother asked.

Sahana held back the tears. "Yes. That all sounds good."

"Very good," her mother confirmed. "I'm so excited, Sahana. I can't wait to hear how it goes. You can tell me tonight when you come to our family dinner."

Sahana nodded, swallowing the prickly knot in her throat. "I should go now. I need to get back to my room and pack."

Her mother paused. "Get back to your room? Why, where are you?"

Sahana's voice caught in her throat. "I was out. I lost track of where I was. But now I'm heading back."

Chapter Twenty

WHEN SHE'D SAID goodbye to her mother, Sahana settled into the wicker chair on the porch. The morning mist had almost melted under the warm sunrays, clearing her view up so she could now see the open meadows lined by trees and the harbor a little distance away. Her stomach was in a knot and her head throbbed as she tried to summon her courage and her thoughts to face Ryan. He didn't keep her waiting and appeared shortly after with two steaming cups of coffee. He smiled, handing her one, and settled into the chair right next to hers.

She sipped the coffee with her eyes closed. For a second, it relieved the stress. But the pleasure was too short-lived to savor. She turned to Ryan. "I'm checking out today," she said, deciding to begin with the basic facts.

He took a sip from his cup and nodded. "I know, and I've been thinking about it. I thought you and I could head to Gig Harbor downtown before you leave and grab some breakfast? I know this really great place by the water. I'll make sure I bring us back in time for you to check out. And I'm sure you've got a busy week ahead, but I want to see you again. I was hoping we could grab dinner together Tuesday and—"

"I can't Ryan," she interjected. "I can't do any of that."

She was afraid to meet his gaze. But still, she turned. A look of puzzlement glazed his face. He shrugged. "Why not?"

Sahana pondered her next words as she interlocked her sweaty palms. "Do you remember Darsh Malhotra?"

Ryan was sipping his coffee. But her words caused him to peel the cup away from his lips. He set it on the table before them. "Yeah, the guy who called you yesterday…the one your mother was going to set you up with?"

"Yes, well. She has. In fact, I'm meeting him at the inn today. We're going to grab a bite after I check out." She stopped to breathe in, only because her heart felt like it would gallop right out of her chest. The look on Ryan's face did not help her heart situation in any way. A dreadfully blank expression clouded his face.

"What do you mean?" Ryan asked, frowning. "And what about this—us?" he asked, gesturing between them. "What about last night?"

Sahana placed her coffee on the table and turned to him. "Look, last night was amazing and I enjoyed every minute of it with you, Ryan. But you've got to understand, I can't waste time on a relationship right now."

His gaze narrowed. "*Waste time?* You think last night was a waste of your time?"

Sahana sighed. "That's not what I said."

He shook his head. "It's what you meant."

"I can't argue with you about semantics," Sahana replied, exasperatedly. "I've always been honest with you, Ryan. I need to get married. I've dated around and I've had relationships but I'm no longer in that place where I can do that anymore. Darsh is looking for a wife, and I'm looking for a husband. If I like him today and he likes me, we're going to move forward in that direction."

Ryan turned away from her, pensively running his fingers through his hair. "I-I can't believe you, Sahana. I mean I'm crazy about you, can't you see that? Doesn't that matter?" He looked back at her and reached out to hold her hand. "You know we get along. You know we've got something here that's special. Isn't that more important than your plans?"

Her hands felt secure in his as he held them. She didn't want to pull away. But she did in the end. "You and I may be compatible. But we're different. You said it the other night, remember? We think differently. You go with your instinct, and I like to map my plans out. Darsh or someone like him was always part of my plan, Ryan."

"I'm not asking you to change your plans," he said. His eyes took her in, leaving a trail of goose bumps on her skin. "I'm asking you to factor me into them."

Tears stung the back of her eyes. She couldn't bear to cry before him. Her emotions were on the brink as it was. She was afraid they'd tip over onto the wrong side again. She stood up to leave, but realized she was still wearing his sweater. She slowly slipped it off her body and reached it across to him.

But he ignored the offering. Standing up tall, he walked up and held her by the waist. "Don't do it, Sahana. Please? Just...please, stay." His words—the way he looked at her as he spoke them, threatened to shake her resolve. She turned away. Placing the folded sweater on the arm of the couch, she reentered his house to gather the rest of her clothes. She caught glimpses of Ryan as he stayed on the porch. When she came back out to leave, however, he wasn't there anymore.

⁓

IT WAS THE longest walk of Sahana's life, from Ryan's family home to The Wildling Inn. It didn't help that she couldn't see where she was going, her vision blurred by tears. When she finally made it back to her room she robotically packed her things up into her suitcase. Finally, she took one last look around. She felt sick to her stomach as various things in the room reminded her of him—the bed where they'd eaten pie, the television with the Bollywood channel, the space in-between where they'd danced and where he'd lifted her up. A soft laugh escaped her, along with a tear. She made her way over to the window where she'd spotted him chopping wood. She stared at its present emptiness, and the ax that was stuck on the flat top of the log. She couldn't understand it. The plans she'd laid out for herself hadn't changed, and yet all of a sudden it felt as if she was swimming against the tide. Her heart refused to get with the program. Ryan had taken center stage. There was no denying that she'd fallen for him. But why was she finding it so hard to get her emotions back on track? "Give it time," she told herself. Maybe that's what both she and Ryan needed.

Her phone rang and she absently reached for it. "Hello?"

"Sahana? Hey, it's Darsh," came the caller's voice.

She paused. "Oh, yeah, hi. How're you?"

"I'm good. I wanted to call to let you know I'm about

ten minutes away from The Wildling Inn. I hope you don't mind meeting me so spontaneously? I know you're probably busy with checkout. Your mom said you'd be okay."

"No, I don't mind. I'm almost done packing, so I'll meet you in the lobby."

"Great," Darsh said. "See you in a bit."

Signing off, Sahana marched herself over to the bathroom mirror. Staring at her reflection, she tried to manually inject some excitement into herself. Darsh sounded great on the phone, and she needed to give this meeting her best shot, if not for her own sake, then for her mother's. Her feelings for Ryan had to take a backseat for now.

Sahana defiantly pulled out a velvety-scarlet lipstick. It was the one that went best with her skin tone. She gave her lips a generous coating and gave her lashes some mascara love. She intended to be the best version of herself for Darsh. Her instinct had tripped her up once. She wasn't about to let it happen again.

HEADING TO THE front desk, Sahana handed her room keys to Holly. She was prepared to run into Ryan somewhere along the way, but she hadn't spotted him yet.

"I hope you had a good time?" Holly asked.

"I did," Sahana said, her eyes involuntarily searching for Ryan.

"It was really nice to meet you, Sahana," Holly said, walking around to give her a hug.

"Likewise," Sahana replied, holding the stinging tears at

bay.

At that very moment, the entry door to the inn opened and Sahana turned. For a second, she thought it was Ryan, but another man walked in. He was not as tall as Ryan, not as broad-shouldered. But he had a pleasant face, and cheerful eyes. He wore a pale blue shirt, under a V-neck sweater, paired with a pair of dark jeans. "Sahana?" he said when he saw her by the reception.

She recognized him from the picture. "Darsh? Hi, it's nice to meet you," she said, extending her hand to him which he shook warmly. Following a quick chat, she led him toward the dining room.

"This is a great place," he noted as they walked. "It's funny, my family owns a summer home in Bremerton which we visit pretty regularly, but I've never heard of this inn before."

"Yes, it's a hidden jewel," she said, almost cautiously, as if not to stir up any of her own emotions that were tied to it.

They entered the partly full restaurant and a seating host walked up to them. He was one of Ryan's cousins, Chase, who appeared to be helping out that day. He recognized Sahana and they exchanged a pleasant greeting before he led her and Darsh over to a corner table by a window, overlooking the orchards. "Wow, that's beautiful. Thank you," Darsh said to Chase, who smiled and handed them a couple of menus to study.

"Can I get you both started on some drinks?" Chase asked.

"Water's good for me," Sahana said. She didn't have an appetite.

"Same for me," Darsh said, his eyes wandering over to her. He smiled and she smiled back. It was awkward but sweet.

"Great, I'll leave you to browse our menu and be back in a few," Chase said with a smile and walked away.

"I know it's a bit weird," Darsh said. "I've been a pawn in my mother's matchmaking efforts many times, but I don't think the cringe-factor ever diminishes."

Sahana smiled. "I know what you mean."

"But I'm excited to meet you," he added. "And I heard you're a corporate attorney like I am?"

"Yes," she said, pretending to read the menu. "What firm do you work for?"

"Barkley and Pack."

"Nice." *A multi-million-dollar business.*

"It can be a stressful job. People don't usually understand that. All they see is the glamour and the lifestyle that goes with it. But it's why I've had to resort to my mother's matchmaking...I haven't had the time to invest into finding a partner."

Sahana let out a dry chuckle. "That sounds like my story. People don't quite get what we do," she said, her eyes catching the outline of Chase as he approached them. But she focused on Darsh for the moment. He was turning out better than she'd envisioned. When the host finally appeared by their table, Sahana turned to him only to have her heart freeze over. It wasn't Chase standing before her. It was Ryan. He looked surprisingly placid, as he held a notepad and pencil in his hand. "Are you ready to order?" he asked her.

Her stomach was a knot, her heart was a riot. She quickly

summoned a bunch of words. "Cesar salad, dressing on the side, no cheese." Ryan didn't flinch as he tore his gaze away from her to focus on Darsh.

"I'll have your Portabella sandwich, with the side salad. Thanks," he said, handing his menu back to Ryan.

But the man shook his head. "We're fresh out of Portabella."

Sahana frowned up at Ryan. He wasn't looking at her, but was communicating loud and clear. She could feel it in her core. She turned to Darsh who was now restudying the menu.

"Okay, I'll have the Havarti and sundried tomato sandwich."

Ryan shook his head again. "We're fresh out of the Havarti—"

"Ryan!" Sahana closed her eyes meditatively. Her head was throbbing, her heart was a mess, and yes, he was mad at her, and maybe she deserved it, but this was no way for him to toy with her.

She looked up at him and he stared down at her, without batting an eye. He turned to Darsh again. "We may have some in the back," he amended.

They handed back their menus to Ryan and he stomped off. *God, what a nightmare.*

"Am I missing something?" Darsh asked, looking in Ryan's direction and back at her.

She sighed. "No, it's just that he and I…we had a thing. But it's over now."

To her relief, Darsh smiled. "Oh, don't worry about it. It's not like you knew when you were going to meet me and to be honest, I just ended a relationship myself. It wasn't pleasant, and I guess that's why I was eager to meet you. I'm done with dating around. I don't have time for that. And this whole arranged marriage idea used to scare me at first, but now I feel like maybe it's not such a bad option. It's how my parents met and they've been married thirty-three years."

Sahana managed a smile. "And mine. And my grandparents before them."

Darsh shrugged. "I guess there must be a method to their madness. Love doesn't have to be the starting point of a marriage."

Sahana nodded. It all technically made sense. All she needed to do was convince herself of it. They talked some more about work and their families. The conversation didn't feel life-changing, but ironically, Sahana knew it would change her life. Darsh felt surprisingly normal. He was funny, although he didn't make her laugh the way Ryan did. He was sweet, yet he didn't cause her skin to tingle the way Ryan did. He was thoughtful, but his words didn't pull at her heartstrings like Ryan's had. But Darsh carried her mother's stamp of approval. He wanted the same thing she did—to get married and settle down.

Ryan now reentered the room, as if attempting to test her resolve once more. He walked over to another table, leaving Chase to bring their plates. He glanced across the room at her for a second before walking out the exit door as if for good.

When Sahana and Darsh were done with their lunch, he paid their tab. "I insist," he said, gallantly pulling out his wallet. "I hope we can meet again?" he added.

"Absolutely." She smiled, walking him to the lobby.

"I'll call you and we can plan something," he said, walking out of the inn, toward his car—a Mercedes just like hers.

"I'd like that," Sahana replied, just as she heard the sound of wood being chopped in the distance. She waved goodbye to Darsh and when his car was out of sight, she rushed down the steps toward the sound which led her to the woodshed. But she arrived to find the space empty. Ryan wasn't there. Had she imagined it? Sahana closed her eyes and let out a sigh. Maybe it was time for her to return to reality. It was time to go home.

But just as she began to enter the inn, she spotted Ryan. He was loading his bike into his pickup truck. Before she could talk herself out of it, she'd called out to him. He turned in her direction and for an instant, she thought she saw a sprinkle of delight in his eyes. But it was gone, as if she'd imagined that, too, like the sound of him chopping wood.

"Are you leaving?" she asked him as she approached.

"I'm going for a bike ride," he replied, curtly.

"I'm all checked out. I'm getting ready to leave, too."

He nodded. "Drive safe." He walked around the truck over to the driver's side and started to get in.

"Ryan, I'm sorry," she said, catching him halfway through the act.

He shut the door, turned and walked up to her. "What are you sorry about? Me? What happened between us, or that guy? Are you sorry you met him?"

She frowned. "It wasn't my intention to hurt your feelings. I got carried away last night and I should've thought it through."

Ryan laughed sarcastically. "You know your problem, Sahana? You think you can plan your entire life out. You can, sometimes. But there are times when you need to trust your heart...your instincts."

Sahana felt the warm blood rush to her brain. "I am who I am, Ryan. And you don't know what it's like to be me. So don't act like you do. You haven't been at family gatherings where you're the sole topic of conversation...with relatives taking apart your love life like a freakin' book club discussion, because they can't understand why you're not married. I've been there," she said, choking on her tears. "It's not a fun place to be. You don't know how that feels, so don't bullshit me about instinct and gut feelings." She paused to massage the tension in her forehead. "I'm tired of being a topic of conversation. I want that perfect life—career, husband, kids. I want that."

"Getting everything you want exactly when you want it doesn't guarantee happiness, Sahana," Ryan replied.

"I'd stay to argue, but what's the point? You and I will never see eye to eye on this." Sahana paused. "I just hoped we could part as friends."

Ryan's eyes appeared to soften as he looked down at her. "I can't do things halfway. Not when my heart's all in. It's all or nothing with me, and the ball's in your court."

The words sank in, triggering a slew of tears in her which Sahana fought back. She nodded. "I guess that means this is goodbye." She looked up to meet his gaze. "Thanks for everything, Ryan. Good luck with the inn. I know it's in good hands." Turning around, she walked away, determined never to look back.

Chapter Twenty-One

"HOW DID IT go with Darsh?" came her mother's voice through the car speakers connected to her phone.

"He was really nice. I liked him," Sahana replied, keeping her eyes on the road while Ryan continued to fill her brain.

"And do you think he could be the one?"

Drawing breath through her lips, Sahana tried to expel the image of Ryan. "He could be, yes."

"Oh, Krishna, thank you!" her mother cried.

"But I can't say what Darsh is feeling," Sahana added, trying to rein in her mother's excitement.

"Oh, he called me, already."

Sahana pulled up at a four-way stop. "He called you?"

"Yes, he called to thank me for setting up the match date, and he told me he really liked you. He kept complimenting how smart you are, how beautiful you are, how ambitious you are. He was just going gaga over you."

It was her turn to pass the STOP sign. It was her turn to speak. "I-I'm glad to hear that."

"There's a reason why God took so long to bring you to your soul mate, Sahana," her mother said. "God made you so perfect, so naturally, he wanted to find the perfect man for you."

The words threatened tears and Sahana sniffed them in. "Listen, Mom, I'm driving back, so I'll talk to you later, okay?"

"Okay, but are you still coming to our family dinner, tonight?" her mother replied. "All your cousins will be there, including Shaan and Misha."

Regardless of the heartache in her own life, Shaan needed her at that dinner. What he didn't know was she needed him that night as much as he needed her. "Yeah, I'll be there."

IT WAS DUSK when Sahana pulled her car into the driveway of her parents' lakefront home in Sammamish. She could see the lights in their living room and the outline of her cousins as they stood inside chatting. It was the usual sight to expect at a Sood-family gathering—the usual crowd. What remained out of place, however, were her emotions. She'd left Gig Harbor feeling unsettled. As if, she'd left a large piece of her spirit behind. She couldn't understand why she felt this way, considering everything had gone according to plan—everything but Ryan. Her match date with Darsh was a success. Her mother loved him, he was very likable, and he seemed to like her. He felt like husband material; someone she could grow to love. But every time she moved toward feeling enthusiastic about Darsh, the memory of Ryan sparred it.

Stepping out of her car, Sahana walked up to the front

door of her parents' home and let herself in with her spare key. But even before she could take her coat off, her mother intercepted her. "Sahana? You're here?"

"Hey Mom," she said, handing her mother a gift bag.

Sharmila looked down at it with surprise. "A gift? That means you're happy with how everything went, no?"

Sahana breathed in. "This one's for Dad," she said, bypassing her mother's comments.

"He'll be so happy. Come, come inside," Sharmila said, leading her daughter in before heading into the kitchen.

"Hey," Mira said with a smile as Sahana entered the living room. She was drinking from a bottle of sparkling water with her husband, Andy's, arm wrapped securely around her waist. It immediately reminded Sahana of Ryan's touch—the way he'd held her when they danced, when they made love, when he saved her from an oncoming car the night they ate chocolates sitting on his truck bed. She felt sick to her stomach but hid it behind a smile. "Hi," she replied, her throat felt parched.

"Mummyji said you were on vacation? Where did you end up going?"

"Gig Harbor and it was a short getaway. Not really a vacation," Sahana replied.

"We thought maybe you heard about your big promotion at work and went off to celebrate by yourself?"

Sahana looked past Mira's shoulder to catch a glimpse of her cousin, Laila, who'd asked the question.

"I haven't got the promotion yet," she replied, as Laila now joined the group with her husband, Hari by her side. Sahana glanced over at her cousins and their significant others. They all looked so happy, so settled. She couldn't help but envy them. It was ironic because her cousins had always told her how lucky they thought she was—how perfect. And now, here she was wishing she could trade with them. Trade happy for perfect.

"Where's Shaan?" Sahana asked trying to shift the focus away from herself.

"I think he's in the kitchen getting a drink," Mira said.

"And Misha?" she asked. "I thought she'd be out and about?"

Laila shook her head. "He said she had a sleepover at a friend's house tonight."

Sahana nodded, wondering if the sleepover had been intentional. Considering Shaan was planning to reveal his recent divorce at the dinner table that night, maybe he'd thought it best to keep Misha out of it. "I'll go see him," Sahana said, walking past her cousins, toward the kitchen.

"Hey, you," she said to Shaan as she approached him. He was standing at the kitchen counter, sipping from a glass of water so she walked over to give him a hug.

He smiled, hugging her back. "Welcome back. How was Gig Harbor?"

"It was okay. I bought something for you and Misha but I left it in the car. I'll give it to you before you leave tonight."

"Thanks, you didn't have to," Shaan said.

"I wanted to."

"But how was the experience overall?" Shaan asked after a pause.

Sahana paused. "Why? Did Ryan call you?"

Shaan looked back, puzzled. "No, I haven't heard from

him." He considered Sahana for a moment. "Why, what happened?"

She breathed in, trying to decide on her next words. She didn't want to talk about Ryan. But knew she was bottled up with emotions. She needed a healthy heart-to-heart, or she'd completely lose her mind. Shaan was the best person for the job. "We...I mean, Ryan and I, we had a thing—a fling...last night."

"Oh wow." Shaan's eyes widened. "I mean I can't say I'm surprised to hear that."

Sahana frowned softly. "What do you mean?"

Shaan smiled. "I mean it was obvious, Sahana. There was this chemistry between you two. I felt it that night at the velodrome and I could tell from the way he'd talk about you to me. He really likes you, you know."

Sahana swallowed the knot in her throat. "He didn't like me when I walked out on him to meet my match date Darsh, I can tell you that."

"But why did you walk out on him?"

"Because I can't date around, Shaan. You know my situation. You know the family...and Mom." She sighed. "But Ryan didn't want to try and understand any of that."

Shaan watched her closely. "Do you love him?"

The question stumped Sahana. Of course, the question tiptoed around in her mind and she'd skillfully evaded it. But facing a one-man jury that was Shaan, was a whole other ballgame. She decided to answer truthfully. "I don't know."

A smile emerged on his face. "That's better than *no*."

"No, it's not, Shaan. I shouldn't have to think about it. I shouldn't be thinking about Ryan." Sahana frowned. "My date with Darsh went really well today. I don't love him, but I feel it could work out with him, and my feelings for Ryan are throwing a monkey wrench into my plans."

Shaan listened for a moment, before speaking softly. "Anita had an affair."

Sahana felt her jaw drop open. "Wait...*what*?"

"With her protégé," he added, his eyes fixed on her. "That's why I left her."

"Oh, Shaan, I'm so sorry," Sahana said.

He shrugged. "You know, I moved mountains for her. I moved countries, went against everyone's advice, including Mummyji and my own parents' who thought I was making a mistake. I was so stubborn about my decision, I didn't stop to think how I really felt about her."

Sahana frowned. "You mean it wasn't love?"

Shaan shook his head. "I realized it as time went by. The affair confirmed it, but by then, it was too late to change reality... It was too late to protect Misha." He paused to look at Sahana. "Don't jump in if you're heart's not in it is what I'm saying."

She stared back at him as his words circled around her head. She said nothing.

THE SOODS SAT around the dinner spread: roti, dal, saag, paneer tikka masala, papadum, rice, raita, with rice pudding for dessert. "You went all out tonight, Mummyji," Mira noted, as she helped her daughter with cutting pieces of roti.

"Yes." Sharmila beamed. "This is the best excuse for me

to do some Punjabi cooking. Otherwise, there is no point in making all these things, if it's just Papaji and me at home," she said, gesturing to her husband who was seated at the other end of the table.

Sahana tried to conjure an appetite as she forked her rice around on her plate. But it was no good, trying. She should've been ravenous, excited to share her successful visit to Gig Harbor and her date with Darsh. But she felt bogged down by the weight of her thoughts, and her memory of Ryan.

"Sahana, you okay?" came her father's voice. She was seated to his left side and close enough that he could likely see the discord in her face. "I thought your trip would've rejuvenated you. But you look tired?" They'd never shared as close a bond as she shared with her mother, likely because he tended to ask the right questions at the wrong time.

"I'm fine. I've got things on my mind," she said, catching the all-knowing look in Shaan's eyes.

"Mummyji said your meeting with Darsh went well. Do you think we'll hear wedding bells soon?" Laila asked.

But before Sahana could reply, her mother jumped in with an answer, ready. "I think we will, at least Darsh seems eager to take things to the next level. You know, I spoke to his mother again today?" she said, now turning from Laila to Sahana. "I'm thinking we should host them here, and we can have a full Punjabi dinner this Friday, what do you say?"

"Yes. That sounds good," Sahana replied robotically.

"Oh, I'm so happy," her mother cried out, clapping her hands with cheer. "This is so exciting, isn't it Vinod?"

"Yes, yes," her father replied with a nod.

"Well, actually," Laila cut in, giving her husband, Hari, a sideways look. "While we're on the subject of good news, Hari and I have some too," she said.

Sahana looked up, her heart beginning to race. Part of her had already guessed what was coming round the bend. A second later, it was confirmed.

"We're pregnant," Laila gushed, as Hari wrapped an arm tight around her.

It shouldn't have felt like a guillotine coming down on her neck, but it did. Sahana tried to mask the feeling under faux excitement. "Wow, a baby on the way. Yay…"

Her mother stood up and walked over to her niece to offer Laila and Hari a hug. "I'm so happy for you two. My gosh, you've come so far, Laila. Do you remember, there was a time when you used to say you didn't believe in marriage, and now here you are, happily married to a pediatrician, and with a baby on the way?" she cried.

"I've had to keep this under my hat all these weeks," Mira added with a laugh. She and Laila had always been close, so this came as no surprise that she was privy to the news before everyone else.

"We called my parents just before we left home, and we're driving over to see Hari's parents after dinner tonight," Laila added.

"Congratulations," Shaan said, as he walked over to give Laila a hug and shake Hari's hand before walking back around to his seat. "Actually, I've got some news, too," he said, sitting down.

"My goodness, what a night of excitement," Sharmila said.

"Well, my news is less exciting than Laila and Hari's, Mummyji. In fact, I wish I didn't have to cast a shadow on by sharing it, but I've held off on telling you all for quite a while and I need to come out and say it."

At this, the atmosphere around the table turned grim, with Sharmila's smile vaporizing. "What is it Shaan?"

"I know I haven't really talked to you all about why Misha and I are back in Seattle. But the truth is, Anita and I are divorced. It all became official, recently and it was fairly quick because Anita didn't contest to gain child custody. Plus, we were married in India, and I was able to hire a really good lawyer who could wrap things up quickly."

Sahana instinctively reached a hand out to offer Shaan a comforting hug.

"So sorry, Shaan," Mira said, followed by the others who offered their sympathies and support.

"The important thing is Misha is safe and happy," Vinod said. "Life takes unexpected turns, and we should learn to turn with it."

"This wasn't unexpected," Sharmila said, cutting her husband short. "I feel for you, Shaan, but I knew Anita was not good enough for you."

"Don't point that out to him, now," Vinod said, trying to ward her off.

"He doesn't mind," Sharmila insisted. "He knows I care about him, don't you, Shaan?"

The gallant man that he was, Shaan nodded. "You tried to warn me, yes."

Sahana shook her head. "But he doesn't need his face rubbed in it, Mom."

This seemed to work, for her mother backed down for the moment.

"Thanks," Shaan said, offering her a smile.

She looked back at him, feeling the sudden sting of tears. "Thanks for letting me pour my heart out," she said.

"I hope it helped?" he said, while the others at the table moved on to chat about Laila's new baby on the way.

Sahana shook her head. "No. But I appreciate it, anyway."

Chapter Twenty-Two

IT WAS A little past nine that evening when Sahana drove into Kirkland's city limits. She turned into her street toward her waterfront apartment. But just as she neared her underground parking garage, she saw a figure sitting on the stairs, just outside her apartment's security gates. She squinted at it because she was sure her mind was playing tricks on her. "Ryan!" she screamed, lowering her car window while her heart jumped in her throat. He'd had his head bowed all this while, but when she called his name, he looked up. She found his truck parked in a street side spot near where he was sitting. She pulled to a stop behind it and got out of her car.

When he saw her he stood up with a smile. "Sahana!"

"What're you doing here?" she cried out, as she walked up to him.

"I wanted to see you. I wanted to talk to you."

He was going to make this hard for her. She knew it. "Ryan, there's really nothing to talk about—"

"Yes, there is. You know there is," he said, gripping her hands. "I refuse to believe you can just walk away from what we had—what we *have*. I can't allow that."

"Why?" she asked, pulling her hands away from his despite how secure they felt in his grasp. "Give me one good reason why you can't let this go."

"I love you," he said, stating the words, clear and plain. "I've loved you since that day I saw you at the inn in your high heels...I remember thinking how fearlessly beautiful you looked. I couldn't take my eyes off you. I tried not to look like an idiot. I tried to hide it, but I doubt I did a good job."

Sahana couldn't feel her legs anymore. Her heart stopped at the sound of his words. She couldn't think—she wasn't even sure she could breath. "Ryan…"

He took a step closer, holding her by the waist like he always liked to do. When she looked up, she could, as always, see herself in his eyes. "I know you, Sahana. I know you like things a certain way. I know it because that's what I love about you…how perfect you are without even trying. I don't know how you feel about me, I don't know if you love me, but I came here to tell you, I want you in my life. I want Sahana Sood, the beautiful, smart, funny, corporate lawyer with a million designer shoes and bags. I want Miss Perfect."

She wanted to speak, but she couldn't feel her lips. "You're asking for something I can't give, Ryan. I can't do it."

Ryan frowned, softly. "Tell me why."

Sahana shook her head. "It's complicated…"

"Then uncomplicate it."

She cupped her face in her hands. "I already told you, Ryan."

"Told me what? That you can't be with me because you want to get married and you don't have time to spend on a relationship? Your mom wants you to marry that Darsh guy who you barely know? You can't be serious?"

"That's not all—"

"What, then?" Ryan cut in.

Sahana let out a sigh, as she stared back at him.

"I'm not leaving here until you tell me," he said, with finality.

Sahana closed her eyes. "God, Ryan, just…go home."

He shook his head. Walking over to a tree, he rested his back against it and tucked his hands in his pockets. "I'm going to wait right here. You can go up and think about it if you like."

Sahana frowned. "For God's sake, will you stop being so stubborn?"

"Nope."

"What do you want me to say?"

He shrugged. "I told you why I want you back. I love you. If I can't have you, I need to know why. I'm not leaving here without an answer."

Sahana pressed her fingers into her temple as a rumble of thunder shook the sky. She looked up at the gray clouds assembling above. She pulled her phone out to check the weather app. Sure enough, it predicted thunderstorms that night. She looked up at Ryan who was leaning against the tree, looking frightfully determined. This was pure insanity. "Are you seriously going to just stand there, forever?"

He considered her insinuation, and shrugged. "Hopefully, it won't be forever."

Sahana frowned. "You think this is funny? They're predicting a major storm tonight."

He smiled. "Good thing I've got my jacket on."

Even in her most perplexing state, Ryan managed to wheedle a tiny smile out of her. She hid it under a frown, of course. But she couldn't help but admire his way with her. "You know what, I've said what I had to say." She turned back to her car. "If you want to stand out here all night, go ahead. It's your life."

"It may be my life. But it means nothing without you in it."

His words had the power to stop her in her track and she turned. He knew he had that power on her. She could tell he knew it. Why else would he be wearing that handsome smile?

Channeling her grit, Sahana walked back to her car and steered it into her underground garage. She headed up to her apartment through the elevator, so she didn't see Ryan on her way up. But as soon as she entered her condo, she walked over to the tree just beneath her balcony. Ryan still stood there. He was looking up in her direction, with no hint of relenting even as the sounds of thunder grew louder and rain began to pour down.

―――

A LOUD CRACK of thunder jolted Sahana awake, and she sat up in bed with a start. She was drenched in sweat as if she'd woken from a bad dream. She looked around the dark room, with a stream of light coming in through the window. She massaged her forehead with her fingers, trying to adjust to reality. She saw a flash of light in her room, followed by a second crack of thunder. A second later, she gasped and dove out of her sheets. She ran up to her balcony to look outside. "Oh, my g—"

She didn't bother to finish her sentence, because she was already on her way out of her condo and out the door—to Ryan, who was still standing under the tree, despite the thunderstorm. The rain threatened to soak her as she stood under the shade just outside the building. A few steps and the security gates lay between her and Ryan, and she called out to him. "Are you out of your mind?!"

He'd spotted her and seemed to have heard her question over the cracks of thunder and pouring rain. He shook his head. "Nope. Just stubborn."

"Go home!" she cried out to him.

He shook his head again. "No can do."

"Argh!" Sahana cried, clenching her fists. She stepped out of the shade, in her pink satin pajamas that did not play well with the rain. They clung to her skin, as did her hair. She ran past the steps, past the security gate, and across the small sidewalk to Ryan.

Standing under the tree before him, dripping rainwater from head to toe, she frowned hard. "I'm going to kick your butt if you don't leave here."

He smiled, instinctively wrapping his arms around her soaking body to ward off the rain. "You know, you look even more beautiful when you're mad and soaking wet."

"It's not funny, Ryan, I mean it. Go home. You've made your point."

"That I'm my father's son?"

She frowned. "You called him pigheaded for it, remember?"

He shrugged. "That was before I realized what love is."

Sahana felt her heartstrings tug. "Ryan..."

"Tell me why I can't have you, Sahana. And please, spare me the bullshit about you wanting to get married and your plans with Darsh, and your nagging relatives. I'm not buying any of that crap. You know there's more. I need to know what it is," he said with finality.

Her eyes took him in. The rain had soaked his hair, his sweater, and jeans, but it hadn't touched the look of determination in his eyes. She smiled because he seemed to know her better than she knew herself—enough, that he'd asked a question she'd never stopped to ask herself. Why did her plans to marry matter so much? More than all the feelings she felt for Ryan?

"I owe it to my mom," she said, allowing the words to surface on her lips. They'd lived inside her all this time and it felt cathartic to finally say them out loud. She looked up at Ryan. "My mother's done a lot for me...me and my sister, Samira. She's sacrificed her happiness, her career, her needs. I've just always felt like I owed her this debt of gratitude...and it's not like she's asking for much, is she? She wants me to get married and have kids and have all the things she had when she was my age. She's watched me go from relationship to relationship...from match to match making a spectacle of myself and of her, among our relatives. I'm not going to put her through it anymore. I owe it to my mother to give her want she wants."

Ryan's dropped his gaze. His lips lingered near hers. "Even at the expense of your own happiness?"

Sahana gently pulled his arms away from her. "You

should understand it better than anyone, Ryan. It's exactly why you changed your mind about selling your inn. You felt you owed it to your parents, and you were willing to pay the price. I owe it to my mom to get married and I will, whatever the price."

He looked down into her eyes. "Looks like we're not that different after all."

"I guess not," she replied with a smile. "And I'm sure if we give it time, we'll both get over it…whatever we had between us."

Ryan let out a soft laugh. "You may get over. I know I never will."

Sahana stayed under the tree a bit longer. She watched as Ryan got in his truck and drove away while the rain continued to pour. She walked back to her condo, changed into new, dry pajamas, and got back into bed. But for the rest of that night, she stayed awake, watching the thunderstorm play out.

Chapter Twenty-Three

IT WAS UNLIKE anything she'd ever felt. But when Sahana woke up the next morning from a night of tossing and little to no sleep, she felt ill. It was as if her heart had the flu. It ached for Ryan. She thought she'd be over him by now, or at least well on her way there. But she felt worse that morning than she had the night before when he'd left. The thought of him was like quicksand, the more she fought to keep it at bay, the deeper she sank. She needed to get out of bed and get dressed for work but the thought made her sick to her stomach. She hadn't chosen an outfit to wear like she usually did the night before. She felt no spunk at the thought of seeing James and Candace. Even the prospect of uncovering whether there was any news from the board on her promotion provided little oxygen to her brain. In the end, she called in sick. She turned her phone on silent and spend the rest of the day in bed, watching Bollywood movies.

By noon, Sahana was sure she'd have a nervous breakdown if she stayed home any longer. Deciding she needed fresh air, she went down for a walk. But the outing landed her in her underground garage and before she could stop herself, she was driving toward Redmond—toward the Mac Quint Velodrome. She spent the morning sitting on the sloping grass, watching the empty tracks. Tears stung the back of her eyes, and she fought them valiantly before they overpowered her and rolled down her cheeks. She knew she shouldn't but she made her way to Thai Bong Tok. She asked for the table where she'd sat the night of her disastrous date with Purab. She ordered some bubble tea. But she never drank it. Instead, she sat staring blankly at the seat to her left where Ryan had sat asking Purab for brochures to create a diversion. She let out an involuntary laugh, despite the tears that trickled down along with it.

THE NEXT MORNING, however, Sahana got out of bed with a sense of purpose. She still missed Ryan; her feelings for him still held together like concrete. But she was determined to work through it to find some semblance of happiness, whether or not her heart agreed with the plan. She went into the office an hour earlier than usual. Work had always been the best distraction for her struggles in life, even when she was younger. She turned to it again, now, even though her career hadn't turned out to be everything she'd hoped.

As she approached the reception desk at Yoland and Wiseman, Sahana smiled at Marissa.

"Good morning," she said, despite the weight of her inner spirit. But before Marissa could respond, Sahana heard James's voice. He was rushing toward her.

"Sahana, I'm so glad you're in! I have something to tell you," he said between pants, pausing to consider the look on her face. "My God, are you okay? I thought you'd be refreshed after your getaway?" he asked, as the two of them began making their way down the hall.

"I'm fine." She nodded, opening the glass door to walk into her office. She hadn't made peace with her situation yet. So, she couldn't bring herself to tell James. "What did you want to tell me?"

James watched her settle down into her chair. "George asked me to set up a one-on-one meeting for you and him today."

Sahana was midway through logging into her machine. She paused and turned to him. Her heart was now beginning to race. "Did he mention why?"

James shook his head. "He said it was important and that he wanted to meet with you before he left on his Caribbean cruise with his wife."

"When's the meeting?"

"One o' clock," James replied.

Sahana checked the time and breathed out. "Okay." This could be it—the moment of truth. The moment that could reveal whether or not she'd got the promotion. The thought sent a wave of adrenaline through her body. Along with it, came the memory of Ryan's comforting voice in her head. *I'm rooting for you...I'm always rooting for you.*

James frowned softly. "Are you sure you're okay, Sahana?" he asked her softly. "Did the trip to Gig Harbor—um, things with Ryan not go well?"

She shook her head. "It went well. But it ended badly," she admitted. "But I don't feel like talking about it." She stifled her tears and turned to the two gift bags she'd brought into work. She handed one to James. "This is for you," she replied.

He smiled, although his brows looked furrowed with concern. He slowly opened the cardboard box and pulled the scarf out. He looked up, appearing pleased yet unsettled. "This is beautiful. Thank you," he said slowly.

"I have one for Candace. I'll give it to her when I see her."

James nodded as if with understanding. He turned to leave but paused just shy of exiting her office. "It'll be okay, Sahana. It'll all be okay."

His words both comforted and gutted her. She nodded. "Thanks, James."

⁓

WHEN SHE ENTERED his office at the top of the hour, George was polishing the rim of one of his paintings on the wall. He turned when he saw her enter and gestured for her to take a seat.

"How're you today? I heard you were out sick?" he asked her, as she chose a chair across from him. George followed suit, taking the seat across from her.

"I was a bit under the weather. But I'm glad to be back, thank you, George."

He nodded. "I'm glad to hear that and I won't beat about the bush. I called you in here because the board has made its decision with regards to the junior partner role at the firm. I can tell you it was not an easy decision for us to make…given you and Walter were both strong contenders. The members expressed varying opinions on the matter of who we think would fill the position best."

Sahana breathed in. She couldn't gauge the undertone of George's statements—if there was good news or bad news beneath it.

Leaning back in his chair, he pursed his lips thoughtfully, as if pausing to study Sahana for a moment. "You know, my wife and I've had the same housekeeper since we were married. Betty Fiore, her name is. My wife hired her back in 1968. What's interesting, though, is that she's not always perfect in what she does."

Sahana frowned, trying to grasp the relevance of this information. Given her head presently felt like it weighed a ton, this was a hard thing to do. "I see," she said, safely.

"She's not perfect, but she's diligent."

"Right," Sahana said with a nod. She had no idea where George was going. But knowing him, he, no doubt, had a destination in mind.

"Which is why the board and I have decided to give the junior partnership, to you, Sahana," he said.

She sat frozen, unable to move or speak.

"This also means you get a nice enough budget to promote James to associate, which I know you're keen to do," he added.

"T-thank you so much, George..." Sahana stuttered.

George nodded. "It's an important role, but I know—the board knows—you will do it justice." The words floated around in her head as Sahana managed a smile. "Thank you, George. I value the opportunity and I won't let you down."

"I know you won't." He smiled back.

Walking back to her office, Sahana stopped by Candace's

and James's desks to share her news. James was especially thrilled when she told him about her intentions to make him an associate at the firm. "I can't wait to tell Ethan," he beamed, hugging Sahana as tight as he could. "Is this perfection, or what?"

Sahana smiled. It was perfection. Every box on her planned list was either checked or nearly checked. She was now a junior partner at her firm, she'd met a man on a matrimonial date that had turned out to be a roaring success, enough that all signs pointed to an engagement ceremony followed by a wedding down the line. Then why wasn't she happy? Why did the thought of Ryan dwarf every other positive emotion inside her? She didn't understand this. James and Candace offered to take her out for drinks to celebrate her promotion but she politely refused.

She returned to her office and tried to immerse herself in her work. But now even work couldn't keep Ryan off her mind. It couldn't save the sinking sensation she carried in her gut. By noon, Sahana gave up on herself. She took the rest of the day off and went home.

Sitting on her balcony that afternoon, with the sunrays tingling her skin, she stared blankly at the tree under her condo that Ryan had stood under, where he'd told her he loved her. He'd said he'd never get over it but that maybe she would. She wondered now, if maybe he was wrong. She'd thought she'd get over it. But maybe she never would, because like him, she, too, was in lo—

Sahana felt her heart stop as the realization struck her like a lightning bolt. *Oh my God...I love Ryan.* It felt like an epiphany. But it also felt wildly familiar. As if the truth has been quietly living inside her all this while and had now made itself known.

She stood up from her chair and began pacing. Her realization had come with a sense of relief. It was as if a blindfold had been taken off her; a fog had lifted to let in the sunlight. But along with this feeling, came a sense of urgency. She wanted to call Ryan—now, now, now. She wanted to hear his voice. She wanted to tell him how she felt—what her instincts had been screaming out loud since the moment she'd met him. She wished, now, she'd listened to them. Walking over to her phone, she picked it up and pulled Ryan's number from her contacts list. Her thumb hovered over his name as she tried to align her thoughts and what she would say to him. But she stopped. What she needed to say to him was important. It needed to be said in person. And her mother? Sahana covered her face with her palms. She needed to see her mother. It didn't matter when her feelings for Ryan were unclear. But now, more than anything else she owed her mother, Sahana knew she owed her the truth.

THE DRIVE TO Gig Harbor felt like the longest of Sahana's life. Every traffic light, every stop sign, every pause felt like an eternity. It was odd how one decision—what felt to her like the right decision, had such a deep impact on her. It had the power to make a cloudy day, like the one that day, feel sunny. Everything around her felt happy. All she needed now was for Ryan not to have changed his mind about her. *Good thoughts, good thoughts, good thoughts...*

Pulling into the parking lot, she rushed out of her car, across the pebbled parking lot and into the inn. She didn't recognize the man standing behind the front desk. There was no one else waiting in line so she walked up. "Hello," she said. "I'm looking for Ryan Mehra, please?"

"Ryan's not in," the man replied.

"Not in?" Sahana frowned. "Do you know where he is?"

The man shook his head. "Sorry, I'm new here."

"Oh er, do you know if Clive or Sigi are here?" Sahana asked him.

The man sported a confused frown and shook his head. "Sorry."

"No, that's okay," Sahana said, pressing her palm to her forehead. Maybe calling Ryan was the better option. She pulled her phone out and began making her way toward his house. Her call went to his voicemail and when she got to his house, it looked like he wasn't home. She called him again, and this time, she left him a message, "Ryan? Ryan, I need to see you. I need to talk to you and I need to see you, will you please, please call me as soon as you get this message?" She realized how desperate it sounded. But she realized she *was* desperate.

She hung around the inn a bit longer, hoping Ryan would show. When her cell rang, she nearly jumped out of her skin. She shuffled to find the device in her bag, hoping it was Ryan calling her back. But it was her mother. "Mom?"

"Sahana? Are you at work?" she asked.

"No, I'm..." She paused. "I'm not, but I'm glad you called. I need to talk to you. Can I come see you tonight?"

Her mother remained silent for a moment. "That is why

I called you, too, Sahana. I want you to come over to the house tonight," she replied. She sounded mellower than usual.

"Are you okay, Mom? Are you not feeling well?" Sahana asked with a pang of concern.

"No. But I will feel better after I see you, tonight," her mother replied. "Come at about five. And wear a nice sari."

Sahana frowned. "A nice sari? Why?"

"I can't explain. But you will understand when you come here."

Chapter Twenty-Four

SAHANA STOOD OUTSIDE the door of her parents' home, twiddling her thumbs, but not ringing the doorbell, yet. She was preparing her conversation with her mother in her head. She had no idea what she would say, but she knew this was going to be the hardest conversation of her life. She checked her phone to see if Ryan had called her back yet. He hadn't. She'd continued to call him and leave him messages since she left the inn. By now, she was afraid of facing the fact that maybe he'd moved on. But her heart was now his, whether he wanted it or not. She therefore couldn't give it to Darsh or any other man. And it was this that she needed her mother to understand tonight.

Reaching her hand out, she rang the doorbell. Her mother answered at the first ring. When she opened the door to Sahana, her mother paused to look at her daughter in her turquoise sari with pink rose patterns on it. She had on a pair of traditional *jhumka* earrings, a *bindi*, centered in the middle of her brow, and some light makeup on. "You look beautiful," she said, and for a moment Sahana thought she detected the glint of tears in her eyes.

"Come in," she said, leading Sahana in.

"Mom, can we sit down somewhere? I'm not sure why

you asked me to wear a sari... I don't know if you've planned something with Darsh—"

"No," her mother interrupted to say. "I have not planned anything with Darsh."

"Then can we talk, first?" Sahana asked.

Her mom appeared unusually sedate. She nodded as they entered the living room.

Sahana watched her with a frown. Something did not feel right with her mother. She was not her usual, overly excited self. "Are you sure you're feeling okay?" Sahana asked her.

"I'm fine," her mother replied, sitting down. She patted the seat next to her on the couch. "Shall I make some chai for us?"

"No, I—" Sahana looked around briefly. "Is Dad around? I need him to hear this, also."

"Vinod?" her mother called out, and a moment later, a head popped in from behind a dividing wall to the kitchen.

"Yes? What it is?" He paused. "Sahana? When did you get here?"

"Just a little while ago, Dad. Listen, could you come in here? I need to talk to you and Mom."

He walked over to take a seat on an armchair next to the couch.

Sahana shifted in her seat. It was her turn to speak again, but now she felt tongue-tied more than ever. "Mom, Dad, there's something I need to tell you both. But before I do, I want you to remember how much I love you, and care about your happiness."

Her father was nodding, but her mother still looked—

well, calm. But it wasn't the kind of calm that rendered others a sense of comfort, no. It felt more like the calm before a storm.

Sahana took a deep breath. "Do you remember Ryan?" she began.

"The one Purab said was your ex?" her mother said, almost without emotion.

"Y-yeah," Sahana replied. "But he wasn't my ex...well, not back then." Her parents sat silent. They didn't say a word. Breathing in again, Sahana now continued to tell them everything about her and Ryan. "I didn't plan any of this. In fact, if you had asked me to guess a few months ago, how my life would've turned out, I wouldn't have been able to tell you." Sahana paused for a moment, to try and assess the damage from her mother's expression.

But Sharmila sat expressionless. "You love him? Ryan Mehra?" she finally asked.

Sahana smiled. "Yes, I do. And I know it's not what you want to hear. I know you like Darsh...I know you hope we'll get married. I wanted to make you happy so bad, I was willing to consider Darsh. But I realized I couldn't...because I love Ryan." Sahana held back her tears. "I love him and he's the one I want."

"You can't make me happy by being unhappy, Sahana," her mother replied softly. "It breaks my heart to think you even considered that option."

She shrugged. "I'm still sorry to put you through it."

Her mother pursed her lips. "What about Ryan?" Her mother frowned. "Does he know how you feel? Have you told him?"

A knot lodged in her throat. She shook her head. "I went over to his inn to talk to him…to tell him I love him, but he wasn't there. I left him messages, but he hasn't called back." Sahana involuntarily picked her phone up to check again. She shook her head again. "He told me he loved me. But maybe I made him wait too long. I feel so stupid because I've been searching for Mr. Right all this time and when he finally shows up, I found a way to lose him again." She could feel the tears brimming in her eyes but she fought to keep them at bay.

Her mother knew, however, to reach out and hug her. Her father followed.

"Do you remember what Mohanji said about your stars?" Sharmila asked. "He said you will find your soul mate this time."

Sahana sniffed back her tears. "I hate to tell you this, Mom, but Mohanji's a liar."

The doorbell rang at the very moment and Sharmila rose to her feet. She looked down at Sahana. "Before you say that, maybe you should answer the door."

FOLLOWING HER PARENTS to the front door of their home, Sahana felt sick to her stomach. She didn't know who her mother had lined up that night. She was in no mood to see a relative or a family friend. She still didn't understand why her mother had asked her to wear a sari. The doorbell rang a second time, and Sharmila nudged Sahana to open it.

Stepping forward, she gingerly reached her hand out.

When she opened the door, she felt her heart stop. "Ryan!" she cried, letting the door fly wide open.

"Hi." Ryan smiled. He was dressed in a traditional Indian *sherwani*—a fancy, embroidered suit made especially for special occasions. Next to him, to his left, stood Sigi, who was wearing a sari, and Clive, who was wearing a kurta. To Ryan's right, stood Suraya Auntie, dressed in a sequined sari, just like Sigi and next to her was her husband, Dilbar, also dressed in a traditional kurta like Clive.

Pressing her palms to her cheeks, Sahana backed away from the door, unable to comprehend what was happening. "I don't understand, I don't get...what's happening?" she muttered.

The others seemed to have each other's confidence, because none of them looked surprised—not even Sharmila or Vinod. In fact, her mother turned to Ryan and his family, and smiled. She suddenly was looking like her old self again. "Come in, please, come in," she said, inviting them in. Sigi and Suraya held silver trays that were draped with a silk cloth so one couldn't tell what lay beneath. Clive and Dilbar each held a silver plate of fruit.

Sharmila led them into the living room while Ryan gently led Sahana into an adjoining study and shut the door. "Ryan, I don't know what's going on here, but I need to talk to you," she said. Her head was spinning. *God, am I dreaming?*

He smiled down at her. "Can I just say how beautiful you look?" he asked her.

The words rekindled her dead spirit like a fire starter to a campfire. "And you look..." She ran her fingers along the gold-thread embroidery of his traditional sherwani. "I've missed you," she concluded, looking up into his eyes. "I went to the inn to find you but you weren't there, and so I called you…" She looked up and frowned. "Why didn't you call me back? And how did you know to come here and—"

"I can explain," Ryan said. "I wasn't at the inn because I was at Aunt Sigi's with the others trying to plan out tonight. I did get your messages, but I needed to talk to you, Sahana. I knew you'd be here tonight."

"But how? How did—when did you plan all this? And with my mother?"

"When you told me you had to marry Darsh to make your mom happy, I realized if I wanted to win you over, I needed to win your mother over first. So, I asked Shaan for her number and I called her."

"Wait—you *what*?" Sahana cried.

"I'm sorry if I crossed the line, but I couldn't give up on you without trying," Ryan said. "I met your parents here and I told them how I felt, and that I loved you, and…" He paused. "I told them I want to marry you."

Sahana felt light-headed, but almost telepathically, she felt Ryan's hand support her waist. "You what?" she asked, her voice coming out a whisper.

"Look, I don't know how you feel about me…if you love me enough that you'll marry me, but I'm willing to wait for you, Sahana. I'll wait for you as long as it takes. I wanted to make my intentions known, tonight. It's why we're here, and it's what I promised your mother I'd do."

She felt the blood rushing to her brain and she smiled. Leaning in, she kissed his lips. "Do you know I got that promotion yesterday? I'm now a junior partner at Yoland and Wiseman."

His eyes widened. "Oh my God!" He reached forward and hugged her tight before taking her lips with his. "I knew you'd get it...I knew it."

She shook her head. "Yes, but the funny thing about it was none of it made me happy. Things were going great with Darsh. But that didn't make me happy either. My perfect plans were working out and yet I was miserable. You were not part of my plans, and yet when you left, you took all my happiness with you and that's when I realized, Ryan...I love you."

A look of surprise glazed his face. "You...Sahana, I—"

"I was wrong," she interjected softly. "I may be Miss Perfect, but I needed a mantra to make me happy...I realized I need to follow my instinct, sometimes."

A smile emerged on his face which bloomed into a laugh, which soon infected Sahana's lips that she started laughing with him. They hugged and he kissed her with what felt like every fiber of his being.

She looked up at him. "Now, I believe you said you had a question for me?"

He laughed, folded himself down on one knee, and pulled a box out of his pocket, which he opened to reveal a stunning engagement ring. "Sahana Sood, will you marry me?"

She got down on the ground with him and kissed him. "Yes, I will, Ryan Mehra!"

TUCKED SAFELY UNDER his arm, Ryan shepherded Sahana back into the family room, where the others were already seated. Plates of samosas, kachoris, hot chai, and pakoras were already set around the table, preplanned by Sahana's mother.

When they entered the room, the others turned to them as if expectantly. Sharmila stood up and walked over to them. "Well?" she asked, looking from Sahana to Ryan and back.

Sahana smiled and showed her mother the ring. At the very moment, a round of cheers erupted. "*Badhai ho, ji, badhai ho!*" they chanted, exchanging hugs, and shaking hands.

They each walked over and gave Sahana and Ryan a hug.

Her mother shed tears of joy as she embraced her. Nor did Sahana attempt to hold back her own. "I'm so sorry about everything, Mom. I wish I'd handled it better."

"Are you happy?" she asked her.

"I'm happier than I've ever been in my life before," she replied.

"Then I'm happy," Sharmila said. She leaned in, to whisper, "Do you know he's part Mehra? Punjabi?" she added, pointing coyly at Ryan who stood talking to her dad.

Sahana laughed. "Yes, his father was."

"I know, Adhar Mehra," her mother said. "Ryan told me everything. He even showed me pictures of the inn. Dad and I will probably stay there sometime."

Sahana smiled and nodded. "What about Darsh? I'm sorry I'm complicating things for you there. I can talk to him and explain everything if you like?"

"Not necessary. I have already reached out to his mother about it. She was not thrilled, but your happiness to me is more important than her happiness," Sharmila said.

Sahana reached forward and hugged her mother as they shed a few more tears.

"This was our mother's ring that Mia wore," Sigi said, pointing to Sahana's finger when the two got talking. "She would've been so happy to see Ryan happy."

Sahana smiled. "Thank you for everything, Sigi," she said, giving her a hug.

The group continued to chat and laugh and eat samosas. Suraya and Sigi unveiled the two draped silver plates. Inside were boxes of jewelry, and one that held a pair of golden bracelets. Suraya and Sigi, along with Dilbar and Clive, extended the trays of fruits and jewelry as representatives of the groom's side, while Sharmila and Vinod accepted the trays, as representatives of the bride. Sharmila picked up a plate of sweets, which everyone, including Ryan and Sahana, helped themselves to, as was the traditional custom whenever good was shared in the family. "*Badhai ho, ji, badhai ho,*" they chanted again. Sahana, still tucked under Ryan's protective arm, watched as Suraya Auntie walked over to her, carrying the jewel box with the pair of golden bracelets. "This is Shagun," she said with a smile. It was custom to give the bride-to-be a piece of heirloom jewelry when an engagement was announced. "This belonged to Adhar's and my great-grandmother," she said, giving the bracelets to Ryan for him to slip onto Sahana's wrist. They fit perfectly.

The others were now free to laugh and socialize. Her father was able to finally break into his whiskey, while the others chatted away excitedly. Sharmila led the conversation, as expected, already discussing wedding plans, and the guest list.

Sahana pulled Ryan away from the group, leading him into the back gardens where they stayed for the better part of that evening, kissing and holding hands.

"You know Ryan, love aside, we need to talk logistics," Sahana said, in between kisses.

"You know I love talking logistics with you," he replied. "Fire away."

Sahana let out a chuckle. "Okay, so I thought, now that I'm junior partner I could ask George if I could work from home a couple of times a week. That way, I won't have to commute from Gig Harbor to Seattle five days a week and we can live in your family home."

He kissed her face, then her neck. "Or we could live closer to Seattle and I could drive to Gig Harbor to manage the inn?" he offered gallantly.

"No," she said, shaking her head. "The inn and the house are part of who you are. I don't want to change that."

He pulled away from her to smile. "Thank you," he said. "On which subject," he added. "I want you to co-own the inn and the house with me."

She looked up at him, surprised. "What? No, Ryan, this is your inheritance. I can't co-own it with you."

He shook his head. "Sorry, it's not open for discussion."

She frowned. "Okay, then I want to invest in the inn."

He was going in for a kiss, but he paused. "What?"

"I want you to own the inn free and clear. I've seen your financial statements, and I know I have enough saved that I can pay us out."

He shook his head. "I can't allow that."

"I'm sorry, it's not open for discussion," Sahana replied with a smile.

Ryan considered her with twinkling eyes. "I suppose we could call it even, now?"

She laughed and he joined in as they continued to kiss, talk, and plan their days ahead under a blanket of stars and a full moon. And to Sahana, the moment, and her life, finally felt happily perfect.

Epilogue

THE WEDDING OF Sahana Sood and Ryan Mehra was one of the grandest events the Sood family had ever hosted. They had two ceremonies—an Indian ceremony at Sahana's parents' house, followed by a traditional American wedding at the inn. Both weddings were quite different and yet perfectly complementary to each other. Sahana wore a beautiful flamingo-pink *lehenga-choli* along with a myriad of family jewels in her Indian wedding. Ryan wore a sherwani and turban. They engaged in a traditional garland exchange, followed by Indian *pheras* or rotations around a sacred fire with their temple priest reciting mantras. The ceremony was followed by a grand reception party at the Four Seasons Hotel. In true Punjabi style, the reception party entailed a night of dancing and Bollywood music fueled by great food, colorful cocktails, and sparkling champagne. The night also witnessed a dance by Ryan and Sahana, a tradition in her Sood family for newlyweds. They chose the same Bollywood song as they'd danced to in their room that night while eating pie. Sahana wore a hot pink sari and Ryan tried to manipulate an umbrella over her head as faux rain fell down on them. The crowd of relatives and friends cheered on wildly as they danced.

"Just don't throw me over your shoulder," Sahana whispered to him as they danced.

"I won't if you admit I'm strong and you're wrong," Ryan said as he twirled her before dipping her backward.

The traditional American wedding took place at the inn, in the back gardens adjoining the apple orchards. Her parents walked Sahana down the aisle. She and Ryan read their own vows. Sahana even wore Mia's gown which Sigi tailored to fit perfectly. It appeared Mia and Sahana had very similar taste, as the gown was exactly what Sahana would've chosen in a bridal dress shop—a vintage off-white lace gown with long sleeves that cupped her wrists, a tapered bodice with a deep-cut V-shaped back.

Midway through getting dressed, Sahana heard a knock on the door of her bridal room.

James went over to open it and returned with a small gift bag which he handed to her. "I believe this is for you. It's from Ryan," he said.

Inside the bag, Sahana found a velvet jewelry box. When she opened it, her heart stopped at the sight of a pair of incredible diamond tear-drop earrings. A handwritten note accompanied it: NOTHING AS PERFECT, NOR AS BEAUTIFUL AS THE WOMAN I'M ABOUT TO MARRY. BUT STILL.

She smiled to herself, holding back her tears as she retrieved the earrings to wear. They naturally went perfectly with her gown.

"My God, he sets a high bar," James said, as he studied the earrings.

Sahana's heart raced with excitement, not nerves, as she walked down the aisle to the processional song. Ryan smiled at her as she did, which felt to her as if he were holding her by the waist through it while her parents walked by her on either side. He looked incredible in his navy tuxedo. Shaan stood next to him. He was Ryan's best man, along with Andy and Hari. Mira, Leila, and Candace were Sahana's bridesmaids and James her bridesman. Misha was the official flower girl and ring bearer along with Mira and Andy's daughter, Anya.

There wasn't a dry eye left among the attendees by the end of the ceremony, following which Sahana tossed her bouquet, which Candace ended up catching. "Alright!" she cried out.

Ryan quietly led Sahana away from the group. "Before we burn the dance floor, Mrs. Mehra, there's one more thing we should do," he said to her.

"What's that Mr. Mehra?" she asked, throwing him a sideway smile.

"Come on, I'll show you…"

Ryan led her over to a tree right by the inn. It was the oldest tree on the property, older than the inn itself. He pulled out a small pocketknife which he used to carve out a heart on the tree trunk and inside it he wrote: R + S.

"How's that?" he asked, turning to Sahana.

She leaned up to kiss him. "Nearly there," she said, gently taking the knife out of his hand. She carved a horizontal figure eight under the initials—the forever symbol. "There," she said. "Now, that's perfect."

The End

Want more? Check out Laila Sood's story in
A Rebel's Mantra!

Join Tule Publishing's newsletter for more great reads and weekly deals!

Sahana Sood's Indian-American Spiced Apple Pie

<u>Ingredients for Filling:</u>

6-7 Granny Smith apples, peeled and sliced (or any other kind of apple that would work well in a pie)

¾ cups packed dark-brown sugar

¼ cup granulated sugar

¼ tsp salt

¼ tsp nutmeg

½ tsp cardamom (or go as nuts with it as you dare)

¼ tsp cinnamon

¼ tsp lemon zest or ¼ tsp lemon juice

¼ tsp chai tea spice (optional)

¼ cup powdered day-old bread (white or whole wheat)

¼ tsp vanilla extract

4 tbsp butter (melted)

<u>Ingredients for Pie Crust:</u>

2 cups all-purpose flour (plus some for rolling out dough)

¾ cups frozen, grated butter

1 tsp salt

1 tsp sugar

6-8 tbsp ice cold water

Method:

Step 1: Prepare Filling

1. Wash, dry, and peel apples before slicing into ¼-inch thick pieces.
2. Into a bowl, add the apples, all the filling spices (including the salt and sugar), along with the butter (melted).
3. Coat the apples with your hands or using a spoon or spatula until fully coated in spice-butter mixture. Cover with cling film and set aside while you work on your crust. Ideally, apples should rest for about 30-60 minutes.

Step 2: Prepare Pie Crust

1. Using hands, combine the flour and shredded butter with ice water (as needed) in a large bowl to create a crumbly dough that can hold together when pinched. Only use as much water as it takes to reach desired dough consistency.
2. Divide mixture into two sections (one for pie base, and the other for pie top or lattice).
3. Be sure not to over-knead the dough as this could cause butter to melt.
4. Chill the dough in a refrigerator, ideally for at least an hour. Note, while Sahana, didn't have this option, this is a recommended step.
5. Once chilled, roll out each section of the dough onto a flat dry surface, to the size of your pie pan, using flour to dust along the way.

6. Line pan with parchment paper and place rolled dough into it, using your fingers to gently press in the edges and bottom to ensure the crust is sitting well inside. Trim the extra dough off edges.

<u>Step 3:</u> Blind Bake Pie Shell (if you have the time. If not, don't worry about it)

1. Line the pie crust with foil or parchment paper.
2. Add evenly distributed pie weights to it such as uncooked beans, uncooked rice, or even sugar.
3. Partially bake for fifteen-twenty minutes in oven at 350 degrees F.
4. This is an optional step to ensure you don't get a soggy-bottom.

<u>Step 4:</u> Fill Your Pie

1. Before placing pie filling into the crust, add powdered bread mixture to the sliced apples. They should have released their juices by now which the bread will absorb to retain the spice flavor.
2. Carefully pour filling mixture into pie crust. Do not overfill and use any leftover filling in a cake or even in pancakes.
3. Place the second rolled-out section on top of the filling and crimp edges using yours pointer and thumb. Be sure to poke holes with a fork on top to allow steam to release as it bakes. Alternatively, you can create a lattice pattern with the section by cutting out equal-sized strips and layering them alternatingly along each row.

Step 5: Bake Pie

1. Bake your pie in a preheated over at 350 degrees F for 45-55 minutes or until you see the pie filling bubbling up on top (if using a lattice method).
2. Allow pie to rest for 10-15 minute before enjoying it along with a good movie, by yourself, with a good friend, or someone you love.

If you enjoyed *A Mantra for Miss Perfect,*
you'll love the next book in…

The Sood Family series

Book 1: *A New Mantra*

Book 2: *A Rebel's Mantra*

Book 3: *A Mantra for Miss Perfect*

Book 4: *A Homecoming Mantra*
Coming in March 2023

Available now at your favorite online retailer!

About the Author

Sapna lives in Seattle, WA with her perfectionist husband and perfect daughter. Her name in Hindi means "dream" and true to its meaning, Sapna finds gratification in dreams and storytelling. She was born in southern India, raised in northern India, and spent the better part of her adult life in the United States. She, therefore, unabashedly clutches her Indian roots while embracing the American in herself. She loves to cook traditional Indian food and, yes, she uses cilantro in practically everything. When she isn't cooking, writing, or being intellectually stumped by her daughter, she may be found running down the nearest trail by her Pacific Northwest home. The inspiration for her debut novel, *A New Mantra*, has been her own journey as both a woman of color and a runner; the latter being a sport that was introduced to her by her husband.

Thank you for reading

A Mantra for Miss Perfect

If you enjoyed this book, you can find more from all our great authors at TulePublishing.com, or from your favorite online retailer.